Obsession at the Opera

Bleu Blanc Rogue
Book 2

Delphine Roy

ARE YOU SIGNED UP FOR DRAGONBLADE'S BLOG?

You'll get the latest news and information on exclusive giveaways, exclusive excerpts, coming releases, sales, free books, cover reveals and more.

Check out our complete list of authors, too!

No spam, no junk. That's a promise!

Sign Up Here

www.dragonbladepublishing.com

Dearest Reader;

Thank you for your support of a small press. At Dragonblade Publishing, we strive to bring you the highest quality Historical Romance from some of the best authors in the business. Without your support, there is no 'us', so we sincerely hope you adore these stories and find some new favorite authors along the way.

Happy Reading!

CEO, Dragonblade Publishing

ADDITIONAL DRAGONBLADE BOOKS BY
AUTHOR DELPHINE ROY

Bleu Blanc Rogue Series
Seduction at the Chateau (Book 1)
Obsession at the Opera (Book 2)

Chapter One

Paris, May 1802

J EROME SAINT YVES strode up Richelieu Street, taking care to avoid the puddles of muck that formed pools over the cobblestones. He usually gave no thought to the state of his boots, but the man he was on his way to see would likely take note of it. Wiser to indulge his acquaintance if it meant a business opportunity in the near future.

He sidestepped another puddle. The heavy spring rains had turned the capital into a veritable swamp. By God, what he wouldn't give to be back home in Chartres instead, in his fragrant garden, instead of traipsing through these filthy streets. But there was money to be made in Paris, and money had no smell. *Pecunia non olet.*

He stopped in front of a tall oak door flanked by two ionic columns, his boots thankfully clean, and pulled the bell. A *majordome* opened. The man squinted, his mouth a severe line, and his eyes aimed right at the frayed hem of Jerome's coat and his threadbare sleeves. Jerome tamped down a flash of irritation and straightened his back. Usually, his imposing frame helped distract from the wear of his clothes.

"Jerome Saint Yves. Monsieur de Marbois is expecting me."

The *majordome* nodded and stepped aside to let him in the entrance hall. "I will inform Monsieur that you have arrived."

Jerome breathed in the scent of polished wood and expensive carpeting. Maybe money did have a smell, after all. He took in the delicate Sevres vase on the rosewood console, the clock with intricate marquetry work in the corner, the newly upholstered set of Louis XIII chairs. The Revolution with all its pillaging and plundering had allowed people like Guillaume de Marbois to make a considerable fortune and buy themselves a good name under the new regime.

Morally reprehensible, perhaps, but as much as it grated him, at the moment Jerome needed work more than he needed principles. Better not think about what his sisters would say about that, after all his stern reminders to never compromise themselves.

"Monsieur de Marbois will see you now."

The *majordome* led Jerome to Marbois's study. Marbois sat behind a large mahogany desk, impeccably dressed in a dark green jacket and matching waistcoat, rifling through some papers. He looked up at Jerome and stood with a smile.

"Saint Yves, how have you been? I haven't seen you in an age."

"Indeed," Jerome replied with a nod of the head. "Not since we finished working on the Théâtre Olympique."

One of the main investors in the project, Marbois had overseen all the plans that Jerome and his colleagues had put forth to complete the backstage facilities and seating area. Marbois's interest had come as a pleasant surprise. The man's coffers might be overflowing, but he was far from an indolent or an imbecile, and their discussions had been most stimulating.

Marbois frowned. "Has it been five months already? By God, time flies. I was hoping to cross paths with you at a play or salon or other, but it seems you've been keeping to yourself."

Jerome shrugged. "I'm afraid the lauded charms of Parisian life are lost on me."

"Ah, but a man cannot subsist on work alone." He held out his hand to invite Jerome to sit, then reached for a decanter of cognac and two glasses. "Or do you have so many projects that you must toil all through the night?"

Far from it, unfortunately. "As it so happens, I've just finished work on a *hôtel particulier*. With the same associates, though I believe it is time for me to take on a more ambitious project."

Rich amber liquid slipped into the glasses like silk. "Which is?"

"I'd like to open my own practice. I believe my skills as an architect will be put to better use."

Not only that, but he was nearing thirty, and by that age his father had been well established as an independent architect. His two sisters were married, and both his brothers-in-law were finding success in their own endeavors. Jerome no longer had to worry about supporting them, as he had for a decade when they'd been exiled in England with nothing but the clothes on their backs.

The exile, the Revolution, the uncertainty and the fear, all of it was behind them now. Paris was expanding, growing like a hungry beast. New streets were being dug every day and houses were popping from the ground like mushrooms. Yes, now was the time.

Marbois raised his glass. "Then we shall drink to your future success. As it happens, I've been giving some thought to having a country estate built in Belleville. I might have mentioned it already."

Precisely. Which was the reason Jerome had immediately answered his summons. "Belleville is a charming village, and you won't have trouble finding available acreage for such a project."

"Indeed, but let us discuss this another time. That's not why I asked you to come today."

Jerome forced his expression to remain impassable and took a sip of cognac. "What for, then?"

"I need your opinion on an antique I'm thinking about acquiring. A piece of jewelry coming in from London."

London. Parks and archways and white towering buildings as grand as palaces. Sinewy streets that reeked of waste and houses that were no better than hovels. Cold and rain and bitter beer the taste of which he had never gotten used to, even though it helped warm his blood and ease his mind when nothing else could.

He did not miss anything about it.

Not a thing? Liar.

Silky black hair spread on a white pillow, soft hands running down his back and circling his chest, and the scent of jasmine, heady enough to make his head spin.

Why must you leave? Can you not stay a bit longer? It is barely even dawn…

He shook the thought away. That single night had been an anomaly, a burst of heat and color and madness in the midst of a gray void.

"I'm far from an expert," he replied carefully.

"Come now, you have an eye for these things. A visual memory unlike any I've encountered. And when I showed you my latest catalog, you demonstrated an impressive knowledge about the origin of each item."

True, Jerome had spent a significant part of his youth poring over the volumes of archaeology and architectural history in his father's library. Paintings and frescoes left him cold, but the idea that someone might take pains in creating something beautiful for daily use never ceased to fascinate him.

He took another sip of cognac. "I'll gladly be of service then. Though if you're going to spend a large amount of money, you might want to ask for a second opinion."

A shrewd smile played on Marbois's lips. "We'll see. This might be the sort of purchase where the fewer people know about it, the better."

Jerome simply nodded. No use questioning Marbois's methods. The man hadn't made his money through profitable investments alone, and was known in the neighborhood of Palais

Royal to have a ledger of buyers from the highest circles of society ready to spend a fortune on rare items, no matter how they had been acquired in the first place.

The *majordome* knocked at the door. "Madame Romano here to see you, Monsieur."

"Perfect. Send her in."

"Madame Romano?" Jerome raised an eyebrow. "I didn't know you were expecting a visit from a lady."

Marbois gave a short laugh. "Whether she can be qualified as a lady remains to be seen."

"If you'd like me to leave and come back later…"

"Oh no, on the contrary. She's the one who wants to sell me this antique. You can see it for yourself."

The footsteps in the hall drew closer, and the *majordome* returned with a woman in a dark gray coat and modest hat. She addressed a stiff curtsy to Marbois, wariness in her dark eyes.

Familiar eyes. Far too familiar.

Jerome's stomach plummeted to his feet and his breath froze in his lungs. He gripped the cognac glass so hard he thought it might burst into shards.

It couldn't be her. Impossible. It had to be someone else, someone with the same plump lips and long lashes and creamy skin. His mind was playing tricks on him.

But then the woman's gaze met his and lit up with the same shock that had seized him. Her lips parted to take in a sharp hiss of air.

This woman's name was not Madame Romano, but Stella Cardinelli.

Stella. A name that had rolled off his tongue again and again as he took his pleasure. A name that had echoed maddeningly in his mind ever since, like clockwork. *Stella, Stella, Stella.*

A name he had done his damnedest to forget, thinking he would never see her again.

Dio santo.

Stella had not known what to expect walking into Guillaume de Marbois's townhouse. She had hoped for a relatively easy transaction, prepared for a difficult negotiation, and braced herself for the possibility that Marbois would offer money for something other than what she currently carried in her reticule. A simple exchange of services, and one she had been taught early to accept as the fastest and easiest means to an end.

But the Palais Royal was not Covent Garden, and for all intents and purposes, she was no longer Stella Cardinelli. She did not know the rules men played by here, and she would rather avoid learning the hard way.

Keep your wits about you. Observe. Do not let him see how desperate you are. But all her self-admonitions and firm resolutions evaporated the instant she entered Marbois's study.

Jerome. What in heaven's name was he doing here?

For a moment, all she could do was stare at him. And not just from shock. Tall and muscular, auburn hair, a square jaw accentuated by a short reddish beard and heavy-lidded gray eyes—he was just as handsome as she remembered. A riveting presence even, just as he'd been at Imogen Barton's party.

Those arms alone—a mason's arms, ones made for lifting timber and stone—were enough to make a woman's head spin and throw caution to the wind. And now that she knew what else they were able to lift...

She averted her eyes, though her heart was still thumping madly. There was no going back to that life. No use reminiscing about that night. Too much depended on her success today to let it all go to waste because the gray eyes that had been haunting her for months just so happened to be staring right back at her.

Oh goodness, what if he told his friend that she was a fraud? No, surely, he wasn't the type of man to...

You don't know what type of man he is. One night means nothing.

Well, she would find out immediately in any case. There was no backing down now.

"Monsieur Marbois, I thank you for granting me some of your time," she said, careful not to sound overly polite but rather like she spoke French in her everyday life. No doubt Marbois would hear a hint of Italian accent, but at least he wouldn't assume she had just arrived in the country.

Marbois gave her a courteous nod and a polished smile, but the glint in his gaze sent a shiver down her spine.

"It is my pleasure, Madame. I don't often entertain such charming company in my home." He turned to Jerome. "This is my... associate, Jerome Saint Yves. He's usually not so tight-lipped, but then again, I don't often get to see him in the presence of the fairer sex."

Jerome's jaw tightened. "Madame."

Stella forced her voice to stay even. "Good day to you, sir."

"Now then," Marbois added. "Show us what you have for sale. Lemieux told me it was quite a sight to be seen."

Monsieur Lemieux owned the antique shop where Stella had first inquired about the possible asking price for the heirloom in her possession. The *cretino* had the gall to offer her a third of what it was worth and bartered haplessly until Stella had slammed her fist down on the table. The real price of the jewel was clearly more than he could pay, but in exchange for a small cut, he'd given her Marbois's direction.

And now she desperately wished she'd never entered that antique shop. As she advanced toward Marbois's desk, Jerome's gaze followed her every movement, and a heated flush enveloped her skin. Any moment now, he could open his mouth and ruin everything. And then what? How would she possibly get by with her funds dwindling?

Clara depends on you. Yes, she must do this, and do it quickly.

She opened her reticule, took out the small box, and set it on the oaken surface. Marbois leaned over it, a small magnifying glass in hand.

"Most impressive. A gold snuff box set with diamonds and mother-of-pearl. And you say it was made by George II's royal jewelers?"

"Yes and given to one of the Tsar's ambassadors as a gift."

"Wouldn't it bear the portrait of the King if that were the case? I don't recognize the person in the miniature."

Jerome approached the table and peered at the box. His arm brushed Stella's side, eliciting a sharp tremor of awareness in her chest. She fought the urge to step away. Or draw closer. Both bad ideas.

"May I?" His deep voice sent a different sort of shiver coursing through her.

"Certainly," Marbois said. "As I told you, I need your expert opinion."

Jerome picked up the box and held it in his palm. It looked tiny in the middle of his large, rugged hands. He took the magnifying glass from Marbois and scrutinized the box in silence.

"This is not the original portrait," he said finally. "There are tiny dents in the gold around it that indicate the original miniature was removed and then another one was put in its place. Given the man's uniform and the style of his beard, I'd say he might be the Russian ambassador."

Marbois shook his head. "That doesn't make sense."

"He might have given it in turn to a lady as a sign of devotion or gratitude. A mistress, perhaps, or one he was courting. And she must have been dear to him indeed, given the worth of such an object."

Stella couldn't help a small smile. "Monsieur Saint Yves is right. This was the possession of one of the court's most celebrated beauties, the Marchioness of Ludlow."

Jerome flipped the box over. "There. She had it engraved with the Ludlow signet."

A hardness in his tone made Stella raise her gaze to meet his once more. Jerome was frowning, his mouth set in a grim line.

His mind was no doubt whirling with theories on how she'd obtained the box. At best, theft. At worst…

She lifted her chin in defiance. *Go ahead and speak if you have anything to say.* Dire straits had simply pressed her into action.

Jerome returned the magnifying glass to Marbois and set the box back on the desk. "If your concern is authenticity, I can guarantee that this is worth the asking price."

Marbois raised an eyebrow. "You're certain?"

"You may seek a second opinion as we discussed, but I worked for the Ludlow estate in London. I recognize that signet. And you can see as well as I can that these aren't paste."

"Very well. I know some collectors that would be extremely interested in acquiring this type of antique. Madame Romano, you've already set your price."

More than what Lemieux had offered, but far less than its true value. The cost of discretion. "It is still the same," Stella said. "Just as long as you guarantee it won't be traced back to me."

Marbois laughed lightly. "Fear not, Madame. If I didn't hold to my word in that respect, I would not have nearly as many clients."

"Good. If we are agreed, I will not take more of your time."

He reached into a drawer and took out an envelope. It was all she could do not to snatch it out of his hands. She opened it and quickly counted the banknotes with trembling fingers before slipping it in her reticule, a flood of relief sweeping over her. For now, Clara would be as safe as she could possibly be.

"Are you sure I can't tempt you with a glass of cognac, Madame? There's no need for you to leave in haste."

Her pulse quickened. Was he going to spring a trap, just as she was about to get away? But Marbois simply laughed and shared a look with Jerome as if they were in on the same joke. Jerome's face remained impassive, as if he didn't care either way.

"Quite sure," Stella snapped, suddenly infuriated with the situation. To hell with them both, if they thought she would accept any offer thrown her way. "You are lucky indeed if you can waste the afternoon away in such an idle manner, but I have many duties to attend to."

And with that, she turned on her heel and stalked out of the room. Only when she was on the pavement did she let herself take a deep breath.

Yet it did not slow her heart or calm her nerves. Even if she had bought more time for herself and for Clara, meeting Jerome again served as a stark reminder. She may have put the English Channel behind her, but she still had treacherous waters to navigate if she wanted to escape her past.

Chapter Two

THE RICKETY STAIRS creaked under Stella's feet as she climbed to the second floor of Madame Bernard's house. The staircase reeked of the cabbage soup that the landlady stirred in a huge cauldron every day and offered to the tenants for a small fee. Stella had been staying at Madame Bernard's for a week and had still not gotten used to the acrid smell, or the bitter taste for that matter, but it was better than anything Stella could have cooked herself.

She reached the landing, and the cries of children mingled with the angry shouts of a woman echoed from the door opposite hers. The lodgings here were cheap, and Madame Bernard didn't ask any questions, but the flimsy walls revealed more about the tenants than the tight-lipped mistress of the house.

Stella clutched her reticule against her chest. Her fingers had kept a tight grasp on it since she'd left Marbois's house. Those bank notes meant better lodgings. Nothing like the luxury of Mamma's house, of course, but that didn't matter. All that mattered was for Clara to be somewhere clean and safe and restful, at least until Stella could plan her next move.

She knocked on the door three times, then paused, then two more times. It opened a crack to reveal a sliver of Jane's ruddy, placid face. Jane opened the door wider and Stella entered. The single room was sparsely furnished with a table, two chairs and two beds, but at least Jane had managed to keep it tidy and clean.

"How did you fare, miss?" the young woman asked. "Did everything go well?"

Stella nodded. "I got the money. I will start looking for new lodgings as soon as I can. How is Clara?"

Jane glanced toward a small crib next to her bed. "Sleeping soundly, as you can see. I nursed her not an hour ago."

Jane had acted as Clara's wet nurse since her birth, five months past. Jane's own child, born out of wedlock, had only lived a few days, like so many babes in the more impoverished areas of London. But the girl had a steady, dignified manner, and Stella had offered her a generous sum on the condition that she would follow her to France once she had fully recovered. Luckily, Jane had bonded with Clara immediately, and had shown impressive resilience as they were escaping England, never knowing how far behind Ludlow's men were. More than enough to earn Stella's complete trust.

She tiptoed to the cot and leaned over to look at Clara. She was breathing evenly, her cheeks round and rosy, the soft tufts of hair peeking from underneath her cap a vivid copper shade—the same as the poor girl who had birthed her. May God rest her soul, and show more mercy toward this babe.

Stella grazed Clara's cheeks with the tip of her fingers. *"Dormi bene e sogni belli."*

Then she straightened and opened her reticule and handed the envelope to Jane. The nurse's blue eyes widened as she peered inside.

"Blimey," she exclaimed. "Ain't never seen so many banknotes in me life. Surely that'll be enough to rent us a palace."

"It's not nearly as much as that box was worth, but we'll have enough to last us for a while. I have high hopes that if I find work…"

"Pardon me, miss, but must you really? This ain't enough?"

It might be, for a few months. But then they wouldn't be able to put money aside, and if they ever needed to leave Paris sooner rather than later…

Stella shook her head. "Any additional income would be a boon for us. And for Clara. We left with scarcely more than the clothes on our backs. She will soon need new slips and caps."

Not to mention that she and Jane could also do with a few dresses. Perhaps she could find some suitable second-hand clothes somewhere. At least they would be clean and less travel-worn.

Jane inspected Clara's cap and sighed. "Suppose you're right, miss. This one's already a mite small."

"Luckily, I've secured an audition at the Théâtre Olympique this afternoon. The troupe is still new, and they're looking for singers."

"As you say, miss. Just as long as you think it's safe."

Stella nearly laughed. *Safe.* A fleeting feeling she had only ever experienced on a handful of occasions. When she was little, curled up on the thick crimson carpet at Mamma's feet while she applied powder and rouge to her face. The first time she'd ever stepped onstage and drew breath for the opening notes of her aria. And then, not so long ago, in a rumpled bed with the pale light of dawn filtering through the curtains…

That's all in the past. Don't think about him. But oh, how could she not when his presence still lingered on her skin? Picturing him standing in Marbois's study, silent and stern, made her heart thump and her nerves thrum all over again. And knowing that he was somewhere in this city, lost in a swarming crowd of thousands, and yet so close…

Concentrate. Do what needs to be done.

"Nothing is safe here, Jane." Indeed, they had left safety behind as soon as they'd boarded the stagecoach out of London. "But the stage is where I'm most at ease, and it will be far better than staying inside all day, pacing to and fro."

"Oh, I agree, miss. But I just want to make sure that… well…" She bit her lip and looked down at her feet.

"What is it, Jane?"

"If you meet a gentleman and decide that you're better off without the babe and me."

Stella squeezed her shoulder, resisting the urge to shake her. "Never. Do you hear me? I will never break my word. And certainly not for any pompous *cretino* with money to waste."

And not just because of her promise to Clara's mother, or because she was responsible for Jane and the babe. She simply couldn't go back to that life.

What makes you think you have a choice, cara mia? Mamma's voice echoed in her head. Sweet as a song, dangerous as poison. *You can't afford not to make use of your assets. No woman can, and especially not our kind.*

Stella's resolve hardened. Even if Mamma wasn't here to see it, she would prove her wrong this time.

"I'll be back before nightfall," she told Jane. "Hide the bank-notes under the mattress. And keep the door locked until I return."

JEROME SMOOTHED HIS palms over the plans that one of his associates had given him that morning. When he'd left his old firm, two of the younger architects had followed him, and what they lacked in experience they made up for in ideas.

It was a new century with a brand-new leader at the helm of the Republic. A time for innovation and dusting off old concepts.

Unfortunately, their only client so far was a bourgeois asking for Rococo-style renovations on his house. Why anyone would prefer ostentatious moldings in gold leaf and swirling archways to the clean, pure lines of the Greek masters was beyond his comprehension, but he had no say in the matter.

At a knock, Jerome glanced up from his desk. "Come in."

Reynaud opened the door. As the founder of the firm, Jerome had his own study in the back, while his two colleagues worked in the streetside room and waited on clients. "Are you finished with my plans, Saint Yves?"

"Quite so. These are good. I would make a few changes here and there, but I'd rather discuss them with you first."

"That might have to wait. Guillaume de Marbois is here to see you."

A visit Jerome had been anticipating for the past two weeks, ever since Marbois had mentioned his desire for a country house. Two weeks and four days, to be precise. For better or worse, that particular visit had been seared into his mind, and late at night, once the day's tasks had been completed, his thoughts returned to it, again and again.

What was Stella doing in Paris? Where was she living, and with whom? Why had she left London? And how in God's name had she gotten her hands on that priceless heirloom she had sold to Marbois?

She must be in trouble. Running from the law. Desperate for money. So stark was the contrast with how she'd appeared to him on the night they'd met—a vision in her red silk gown, her graceful neck encircled with three strings of pearls, her dark eyes bold and seductive and her lips curled in an easy smile—that a part of him still wondered if she hadn't indeed been a different person.

But the sharp bursts of heat that her presence provoked in him spoke the truth. No other woman had ever had such an immediate, irrepressible effect on him. As soon as he'd laid eyes on her at Mrs. Barton's party, he had known the temptation would be too strong to resist.

He straightened his cravat and cleared his throat. He had better compose himself before his wandering mind betrayed itself in a visible way.

"Right. You can send him in."

"Do you suppose he came here to discuss his project with you?"

"Only one way to find out."

Reynaud nodded and disappeared. A moment later, Marbois

strolled into the study.

"Nice little storefront you have here," he said in his usual jaunty tone.

Two windows, a door and a sign Reynaud had painted himself. Hopefully their reputation would make up for their modest quarters.

"It's only temporary, until we can afford something bigger." He motioned to the chair in front of his desk. "Take a seat. I'm pleased you decided to pay us a visit."

"I would have come sooner, but I've been dreadfully busy. Thought we might discuss my future house. You took off like a frightened colt when you came to visit."

True. It was all he could do not to curse out loud and slam his fist on the desk as soon as Stella had left. He'd had to excuse himself a few minutes later.

"My apologies. I'm at my leisure now if you want to talk. Have you made your decision?"

"I have. I think we could do good work together, you and I. You're a pragmatic sort, like me. And the men who work for you respect you and trust your opinion."

Satisfaction swept through him, though he was careful to keep his face still. "I'm glad you think so. It might have to do with the fact that I worked as a mason when we were in London. The men respect those who respect their work."

"Which only comforts me in my choice. Now, let me tell you what I had in mind."

For the next while, Marbois described his vision of a country house in Belleville, tall windows and columns, white stone and archways, encased in the luxurious beauty of an English-style garden. A massive undertaking, but Jerome wasn't intimidated, on the contrary. This was the project he'd waited his entire life for. He took page upon page of notes, and when Marbois was finally done, he piled them into a neat stack.

"Very well," he said.

Marbois laughed. "That's it? No comments or suggestions?"

"Those will come when we start drawing up the plans. You'll have to hire someone to see to the gardens as well, but I have a few names to recommend if you haven't decided on anyone yet."

"Coming from you, Saint Yves, I was expecting a rebuff on my more fantastical ideas, like the folly made to look like Greek ruins."

Jerome shrugged. "Those are quite popular nowadays."

"Yes, yes, all of this will be the pinnacle of good taste. But what say we celebrate our future collaboration in a less respectable fashion?"

Mischief glinted in Marbois's gaze. Jerome steeled himself. Was he about to suggest they go visit the ladies of the Palais Royal, or the gaming hells? Surely a man of Marbois's fortune could afford entry in the less seedy venues of the neighborhood, but even so, the thought of losing hard-earned money at cards or worse, paying a woman to service him, inspired nothing but the deepest disgust.

"What do you have in mind?" he asked, keeping his tone even. Now was not the time to vex Marbois by refusing his offer, but God help him, there were certain lines he would not cross.

"They're playing *The Marriage of Figaro* at the Olympique tomorrow night."

Music. That he could certainly enjoy. "One cannot refuse an evening with Mozart."

Marbois smiled. "Yes, but that's only half the entertainment I have planned. I have it on good authority that there are new girls, dancers and singers, just waiting for a gentleman to swoop in and lavish them with gifts."

And no doubt Marbois wouldn't be the only one waiting in the wings. Jerome bit back a sigh. "I didn't know you were on the hunt for a mistress."

"Sooner or later a man feels the need to settle down," Marbois answered, amused. "What about you, Saint Yves? You'll soon be making a good amount of money. One of the girls might want to take a chance on a promising young architect."

Jerome tapped his fingers on the desk impatiently. No use telling Marbois that if he ever settled down, it would only be when he found a respectable woman to be his wife and the mother of his children. It was his duty to uphold the Saint Yves name, and he certainly wouldn't achieve his goal by keeping a mistress. He knew only too well where overindulgence could lead.

How terribly provincial. He could almost hear the words coming out of his companion's mouth if he admitted as much.

"I'll keep that in mind," he simply said. "In the meantime, I'll gladly accompany you to the opera. It'll be nice to see all of our hard work put to use."

Marbois sprang up from his chair and held out his hand for Jerome to shake. "It's done then. I trust you have something to wear?"

Jerome nodded. His sister Honorine had taken pains to sew him an evening jacket and waistcoat from donated fabric three years past, when he'd gone from working as a mason to assisting architects in London. Since they mostly remained in his trunk, they were still in good condition. But as talented and resourceful a seamstress as Honorine was, it was probably a far cry from what Marbois had in mind. Still, it would have to do for now.

"Marvelous," Marbois replied with a wicked grin. "You're all set to join my hunting party."

Chapter Three

J EROME SQUARED HIS shoulders and craned his neck. The railing of the balcony was less than two meters away, but the crush of attendees at the Théâtre Olympique was such that he and Marbois had been working their way to a spot where they could see the stage for half an hour. Jerome's imposing frame had proved useful to get them through, but Marbois kept stopping to chat with acquaintances, men in crisp, colorful evening jackets and silk cravats. The balcony was standing room only, and evidently, being seen and discussing the right topics with the right people was more important than listening to Mozart.

Jerome pushed his way forward impatiently. The hum of voices didn't drown out the musicians and the singers on stage, but damn it all, it was distraction enough.

One dark-haired gentleman with an aquiline nose grabbed Marbois by the arm as they passed. "I say, aren't you going to greet an old friend?"

"Tremblay! I thought I might run into you tonight. You've been a regular here."

"Best stage in the city. Oh, I meant to ask you, how did that deal go through in the end? The one with the case of fine china?"

As they started chatting about antiques, Jerome craned his neck for a glimpse of the stage, but a pair of women in bright organza dresses squeezed in front of him, laughing giddily, and the extravagant plumes in their hair blocked his view entirely. Blast. If he wasn't mistaken, Cherubino's first aria had just started.

Non so più cosa son, cosa faccio, or di foco, ora sono di ghiaccio.

Though he did not speak Italian, he had read a French translation of the libretto and remembered this particular piece, as the lyrics had struck him. *I no longer know what I am, what I do, now I'm all fire, now all ice.*

His sisters would certainly have agreed on his demeanor being too icy. Honorine had often told him that he should not be so stern, and teased him gently in an effort to make him laugh, just like she did her children. And Antonia, bless her, had tried to read him passages of her favorite novels or poetry anthologies in what he assumed was an effort to make him see beyond the tedious grind of their daily life.

"Does this not touch your heart, brother?" she'd asked, her gray eyes wide and soft. "The way Delille describes the eternal splendor of nature?"

In truth, despite Antonia's best efforts, novels and poetry left him cold. Music, on the other hand… There lay the fire.

Signorina Cardinelli, won't you sing a song for us? What a treat it would be for my guests tonight!

Oh, how easily the scene came to his mind when he let it, each detail as vivid as if it had been yesterday. Stella had complied with a dazzling smile to Mrs. Barton's request, and the moment she'd opened her mouth, the aria she'd chosen, from *Orpheus and Eurydice*, had poured into him like liqueur, warming him to the very marrow of his bones, setting his blood aflame.

He'd wanted her then and there, an intense need that crushed his chest and made it hard to breathe. When she'd finished, their eyes had met across the room. And he'd watched, dumbstruck, as Stella picked up her fan and sashayed over to him. Why him, when all the men present were no doubt eager for an introduction? He still couldn't explain it.

I believe we have not yet met, sir. Are you a friend of Imogen's?

A hand clapping onto his shoulder pulled him from his memories. Marbois, of course. He turned.

"Saint Yves, I haven't properly introduced you. This is Jacques Tremblay, a business associate of mine. Jerome Saint Yves is my architect."

Tremblay's gaze flicked over Jerome's worn jacket and plain cravat, and his chin tilted up. "Oh, so you have an architect now?"

"For his country house in Belleville, yes," Jerome replied. "Marbois has trusted me and my colleagues with its design and completion."

The man raised a quizzical brow. "And is he paying you to accompany him to the opera as well?"

Jerome held his gaze and nodded toward the balcony's railing. "See that there? I penciled the original drawing myself when we were working on the Olympique. Would you care to test how solid it is?"

Tremblay burst out laughing and Marbois followed suit. "Well said, *monsieur*. By all means, let us get a closer look at what's happening on stage and test the soundness of your creation."

By the time they had finally shouldered their way to the railing, the Count was trying to seduce Susanna while Cherubino hid behind a chair.

"*Seigneur*, we should have gone directly to my box," Marbois muttered. "It'll take us another hour just to come back the other way."

"It's good for business to be on the balcony," Jerome remarked. "Less than ideal if one actually wants to enjoy the music."

"Come now, don't tell me Marbois invited you here for the music, or for business," Tremblay said with a snort. "Surely that sly bastard has other intentions in mind. What do you think, eh?"

For a moment, all three of them observed the comedic comings and goings of the singers on stage. The woman singing the part of Susanna had a trim waist and honey-colored hair, and she moved with easy grace across the stage.

"I've seen Marcelline Duhamel perform before," Marbois said. "She's a beauty but I hear her asking price is steep. It would cost me an arm and a leg to get between hers."

"And to think, before the Revolution all you needed was your title," Tremblay sighed. "A duke with empty pockets could do better than a wealthy bourgeois."

They watched and listened to the end of the act, then the curtains closed for the entr'acte. A flock of ballerinas in dresses of pale gauze arrived on stage, fluttering to and fro like butterflies as they danced to a lively tune.

"More to your taste, perhaps?" Tremblay asked.

"One only need cast the net," Marbois replied. "And before you give me one of your looks, Saint Yves…"

Jerome held up his hands. "I did not utter a word."

"You don't need to. That's why I said your looks." His face scrunched into a mock frown. "Like this, see? Yes, you're an honorable man from an honorable family, but I'll have you know that the gentlemanly thing to do here is to support these girls as they start their career."

Jerome shook his head but couldn't help a smile. "Yes, you're a real patron of the arts, aren't you?"

Tremblay nudged Marbois. "I'll say. Your last mistress was an actress in the Comédie Française, wasn't she?"

"Right, but the problem with that particular profession is there's always a doubt lingering in one's mind on whether she's playacting in bed as well. Besides, a ballerina might be more… limber."

Jerome leaned over the railing. Good Lord, he didn't know how much more of their bawdy remarks he could take. They were just as crude as his boyhood friends back in Chartres when they bragged about bedding peasant girls.

Flipped up her skirts and took her right there against the oak tree, and after that she was begging for more. Takes almost nothing to get them to spread their legs for you.

Back then, at seventeen, he had been stupid enough to let their words sway him, and it had ended in disaster. At least he'd learned never to listen to that sort of salacious boasting again. Thankfully, the ballerinas finished their dance quickly enough, and a quadrille of male performers replaced them.

Marbois turned away from the stage. "Virginie Poulain is singing the part of the Countess, is she not?"

"Oh, you haven't heard?" Tremblay replied. "Apparently, she's been taken ill. They had to replace her at the last minute."

"Who with?"

"Bianca Romano. She's new to the troupe."

Jerome's fingers gripped the railing. His thoughts began to whirl until dizziness threatened to overwhelm him, and it was all he could do to keep his balance.

"Romano?" Marbois repeated. "Saint Yves, you don't think it's the same woman who sold me the box?"

Stella. Of course, it had to be her.

"I suppose it's possible," he managed to reply.

"Well, if it is, we might as well go greet her after the show while we're backstage."

Jerome clenched his jaw. That was the least of his concerns at the moment. First, he would have to endure three acts of Stella singing on stage, her pure, crystalline voice seeping into him, threatening to undo the constraints he had painstakingly placed on himself since spending the night with her. Constraints that kept everything tightly under control.

His lust. His hunger for things that he did not want to voice, or even contemplate. Things that Stella had coaxed out of him effortlessly, for in her arms he had lost his grasp on reason.

Tell me what it is you most desire. Your secrets will be safe with me.

The curtains opened again and there she was, standing in a dark blue satin gown, her dark hair piled in silky curls and her features sharpened with powder and rouge. The tight bodice of the gown pushed up her breasts, and Jerome let his eyes linger on her sumptuous curves. He couldn't help it. By God, she was the most desirable woman he'd ever laid eyes on.

As soon as she started to sing, the languid notes falling from her lips with exquisite precision, he felt as though he was drowning. The sadness that emanated from her seemed all too real, and though he knew fully well that she was singing about her fictional husband's infidelity, anger at imagining Stella being mistreated by anyone suddenly pounded through his veins.

"It *is* her, isn't it?" Marbois murmured next to him. "Most intriguing. What would an opera singer be running from?"

"Who can tell?" he replied roughly. The last thing he wanted was Marbois sniffing around Stella. Even seeing the man leering at her like he had at those dancers made his blood boil all the more. "You do not happen to have a flask with you, by any chance?"

Marbois grinned and reached inside his jacket for a silver flask. "Well now, that's more like it. Only the finest cognac."

He handed him the flask and Jerome unscrewed the cap to take two long gulps. Replacing one form of intoxication with another, or so he hoped.

STELLA PATTED HER forehead with her handkerchief and inhaled deeply to catch her breath. A strange sort of excitement rushed through her trembling limbs, battling with exhaustion. She reveled in the familiar feeling, in the sensations she had so dearly missed—the thud of shoes on the wooden planks of the stage, the musty smell of the heavy velvet curtain, the joyful brouhaha of voices when the show had gone well.

Oh, how she'd missed this. Even if her nerves were still jangling from the unexpected role she'd had to fill, with only three days to prepare. She'd originally been cast to sing in the chorus and as a possible stand-in for Virginie Poulain, given that she already knew the part of the Countess. However, she hadn't expected her very first performance on the stage of the Olympique to be quite so daunting.

The raucous applause of the audience had been all the sweeter. And for a few glorious hours, she had forgotten the circumstances that had brought her there in the first place.

She walked down the winding backstage corridor to the tiny space she'd been allotted. On her way, she passed Marcelline's dressing room, which was considerably larger. The door was open, and the soprano was daintily picking pins out of her hair in front of the mirror.

"Well done, Bianca," she called to Stella. "You did a perfectly adequate job as the Countess."

Adequate. She had only known Marcelline for two weeks but it was enough to know that she was a master in the art of backhanded insults. Still, it wouldn't do to simply ignore the *prima donna* of the troupe if she wanted to keep her position. She slowed to a stop and forced a smile.

"Thank you, Marcelline. I'm glad I was able to fill in for Virginie."

"Yes, what luck that you already knew the role. You said you sang it for your previous troupe? In Milan?"

"Indeed."

Marcelline turned away from the mirror and gave her a sharp look. "I must say, I cannot imagine why someone would leave La Scala for the Olympique."

Stella forced her expression to remain placid and polite. "One might simply desire a change of scenery."

Before Marcelline could ask any further questions, one of the young male dancers of the troupe arrived, wearing nothing but his trousers and carrying a large bouquet of red roses.

"A gift from Monsieur Girard," he said. "He's waiting in the wings. Shall I tell him you're receiving?"

A look of mild interest passed over Marcelline's face. "First let me see if there's a piece of jewelry hidden in one of the buds. He should know by now that simple flowers won't do."

Stella slid away from the door. Now was the time to retreat into her own dressing room. It was further down the corridor, and little more than a closet, really. But it had a lock, and at least she didn't have to change with the chorus singers and the dancers. She knew full well what sort of antics went on in the main dressing room when gentlemen attendees came to call. They would stride in, arrogant as you please, look over the girls, even touch them as if they were selecting apples from a stall. And the girls would have to smile and simper, hoping a rich patron would make the humiliation worth their while.

Just like Stella had in the past. At least Mamma had taught her never to let a man sample the goods before obtaining compensation. A lesson Clara's poor mother could have benefited from.

Clara. I must get back to her. Stella started to unlace her bodice impatiently, but undressing and taking off the powder and rouge from her face was a tedious process. She was brushing her hair in her chemise and corset when a small rattling sound caught her attention.

She froze, her skin tingling with dreadful awareness. She swallowed painfully before speaking, forcing the tremor out of her voice. "Who's there?"

Silence. Then, a thud and what sounded like a muffled voice.

Pure instinct took over. She grabbed an ivory pin from the tiny dressing table. Not much of a weapon, but she'd be damned if she didn't defend herself.

"Whoever is there, go away immediately," she shouted with more bravado than she felt.

The door crashed open.

A man fell to the floor, and another one on top of him, landing a punch straight to his nose. In the blur of movement, it took her a few seconds to recognize the man on top. Her breath left her lungs all at once.

"Jerome!"

He punched the man again, on the jaw this time. The intruder let out a hoarse cry of pain and spat blood. *Porca miseria*, he was going to kill him. Her voice came out in a wail.

"Jerome, enough!"

He glanced up at her for the briefest moment. But it was enough for the man to shove his chest roughly and throw him off balance. Jerome landed on his side, and the man scrambled out of the room and into the corridor. Jerome jumped to his feet but Stella grabbed his arm.

"Stop it! Stay!" She squeezed her fingers. "Please."

Jerome relented, his chest heaving and his eyes filled with cold rage. A reddish bruise was starting to bloom in his cheekbone.

"What in heaven's name is going on?" Stella asked. "What are you doing here?"

"He was trying to break into your dressing room. Do you know him?"

"No, of course not. I've never seen this man before in my life."

"And you have no idea why he would try to pick the lock of your door?"

Stella's stomach dropped. *Dio santo*, what if Ludlow had sent him? No, impossible. She had been in Paris almost a month now, and had recently moved from Mrs Bernard's dilapidated house to cleaner lodgings. If she had left any tracks despite the meticulous care she had taken since leaving London, surely none were left.

Besides, this would not be the first time a man tried to break into a singer's dressing room, and chances were the man's nefarious purposes were more commonplace. Whatever the case, though, she couldn't tell Jerome. She'd promised to herself that she wouldn't tell a soul what had happened, and put her trust in Jane alone.

"None," she replied. "Perhaps he was just an admirer. Men out there hope for an invitation to one of the girls' dressing rooms."

She looked at him pointedly and Jerome straightened his shoulders. "That's not why I came."

A twinge of disappointment pinched her heart. Under other circumstances, Jerome would have no need for roses or a piece of jewelry to obtain whatever he desired from her. His broad shoulders and chest filled the tiny space, and he stood close enough that she could feel the heat emanating from his body.

So strong and solid. Her palms remembered the feel of his muscles perfectly. Smooth and hard as stone.

"Why did you come, then?" she asked in a low voice, suddenly aware how little she was dressed. A flush rose to her cheeks. Was he remembering as well? His hands and his mouth had certainly taken their fill of her breasts when last they had been alone.

She crossed her arms over her chest but that only seemed to draw Jerome's gaze. Just as quickly, he averted his eyes and kept them firmly fixed over her head. "I will tell you once you are properly attired. And then I will accompany you back to your home."

She shook her head. "No, out of the question. You cannot—"

"If you think for a moment that I'm letting you return to wherever it is you're staying by yourself after what happened, you're gravely mistaken," he retorted. "If you refuse, I will simply follow you the entire way. Right up to your door."

Chapter Four

J EROME HUNCHED ON the narrow seat. With its low ceiling, the coach was too damned small for a man his size, but it might have been less uncomfortable had his companion not sat in utter silence. Instead, they were at their leisure to listen to the rumble of the wheels on the cobblestones all the way down Gramont Street.

Stella was bundled up in the same gray cloak she'd worn to Marbois's house, and her gaze was firmly fixed outside the tiny window, watching the street lamps go by. She kept her mouth pursed and anger swirled in her dark eyes. No matter. He had rather she be furious at him than let her return home unaccompanied.

Especially after catching that wretch who attempted to enter her dressing room. Jerome's blood still roared with the desire to smash the bastard's teeth down his throat. Thank the devil he had followed Marbois and Tremblay backstage.

When he'd found a man in dark street garb in front of Stella's door, trying to pick the lock, his intentions were easy enough to guess. Some of the gentlemen present might try to sway the girls with gifts or promises, but others didn't bother with asking for invitations and chose a more direct approach. Jerome's hands tightened into fists on his knees. By God, he'd wanted to pummel that scoundrel's face to a bloody pulp.

And if the man hadn't been there… What would have happened then? He glanced at Stella again. Being so close to her in such a state of undress, with the fire of the fight still roaring in him, had made it all too easy to imagine that they might take up where they'd left off back in England.

No. He must not let his mind take that path. He must be a better man than those who sought only relief from their baser impulses. Stella needed his help, not his desire.

No matter how strong that desire thumped through his veins.

The coach came to a stop. Jerome grabbed the handle of the door before Stella could reach it, and stepped onto the cobblestones, extending a hand to help her out. Stella grudgingly accepted, but her fine-boned hand slipped away as soon as she found her footing.

Jerome appraised the building. The facade was plain but clean, and the simple, symmetrical lines and high windows pointed to a recent construction. "How long have you been living here?"

Stella moved toward the front door. "Only a few days."

Which meant she must have been staying elsewhere when they'd met at Marbois's house. Had she found a protector in the meantime? A queasy sensation settled in his belly. Confronting a jealous lover who lived with her would be intensely displeasing, true, and it would put Stella in an even more difficult situation.

"Is there any risk to you if I accompany you to your door?" he asked.

Stella looked at him over her shoulder and hesitated for a moment. "To me? None at all. To you, on the other hand…" She gave him a wry smile. "What might persuade you to stay down here?"

"A man with a loaded pistol ready and waiting." Fists, he could certainly handle.

Stella sighed. "Then you are safe. One will find neither man nor pistol in my home."

At her words, a possessive burst of relief coursed through him. He pushed it aside immediately and followed her up a flight of wooden stairs up to the first landing. Stella stopped in front of the door on the left to fish out a pair of keys from her reticule, then she turned to face him.

"Are you satisfied that I will be safe now?"

"Quite so."

"Is that why you came backstage in the first place? To inquire upon my safety?"

Blast. He had failed to explain himself, and hoped that she wouldn't ask again. Because he wasn't sure how to answer.

"I was with Marbois and a friend of his," he replied cautiously. "Marbois has hired me to make the plans of his new country house in Belleville. A certain amount of hobnobbing is expected."

"Hobnobbing." She arched a dark brow. "I see. And you asked for directions to my dressing room?"

He shook his head. "No. No, it wasn't like that. I was waiting for them in the corridor while they… consorted with some of the ladies in the troupe. A dancer asked me if I wanted to see someone in particular and I…"

Thank goodness she could not see the flush rising to his cheeks in the near darkness. He cleared his throat. "I had no idea you were singing at the Olympique. I simply wanted to make sure that you were not in need of assistance."

"A protector, you mean?"

"An ally," he corrected. "Your visit to Marbois's house gave me the impression that you might be in need of one."

She lifted her chin. "Well, as you can see, everything is fine. I have secured a good position at the Olympique and my lodgings are adequate. There is nothing more for you to worry about."

A high-pitched wail came from the other side of the door.

His chest felt as if it had just been plunged in ice cold water. "That sound. Is that…?"

Stella pressed her mouth into a line and closed her eyes for a moment. The sound came again, louder this time. A crying babe.

A babe. Lord in heaven.

Before he could say anything, Stella unlocked the door and slipped inside. He pressed his palm against the door, holding it open. He would be damned if he let her shut him out now.

"Why did you not tell me you had a child?"

She whipped around. "It is none of your concern."

"It *is* my concern if the babe is mine."

A primal, furious instinct took over him. Honorine had given birth to six children, five of them while the family all lived under the same roof in London. He knew perfectly well what an infant sounded like. Mrs. Barton's party had taken place eleven months prior…

Stella opened her mouth to answer, but they were interrupted by the arrival of a woman in a nightgown. She held a candle, the pale flame lighting an even paler face and wispy blonde hair. When she saw Jerome, she froze and glared at him.

"I dunno who ye are," she said in English, her accent rough and thick, "but if ye've 'armed me mistress in any way…"

"It's fine, Jane," Stella replied, switching seamlessly to English. "This is Jerome Saint Yves. An acquaintance, nothing more. He was simply making sure I got home safe from the opera."

"I heard shouting."

"Simply clearing up a small matter. And now Monsieur Saint Yves is free to return home."

Jane nodded. "Good. Clara's due a feeding, but I reckon she'll want ye to hold her for a bit, now that yer back. She fussed all evening."

Clara. Jerome caught Stella's gaze and frowned. *Is she mine?*

She seemed to understand his wordless demand. "Very well, Jane. I will only be a moment."

Jane nodded and dragged her feet back down the hallway. Stella turned back to Jerome, her eyes aflame.

"There is no further reason for you to stay," she said in a calm but firm voice. "You have no obligation toward Clara, not under the law nor in the eyes of God. Is that clear?"

True, they had taken precautions, though they were by no means foolproof. Who *had* sired the babe, then? Some other man she'd dallied with shortly after him? Or even before, though she had not shown any visible sign of being with child? Good God, the very idea… It should not have surprised him, and yet his stomach gave a sickened lurch.

"Perfectly clear," he growled. "I will not burden you with my presence any further. Good night, *madame*."

He turned his heel and left, barely resisting the urge to slam the door behind him.

⇥⟫⟪⇤

REYNAUD SPREAD THE latest drawings on the table and rubbed his chin.

"I think our client will be pleased with the height of the room if he plans to have a fresco painted on the ceiling. As for the stucco, we should ask Massy if his men are available. Don't you agree?"

Jerome studied the crisp lines to force his thoughts back into their conversation and piece together what his associate had just said. *Ceiling. Fresco. Stucco. Massy.* "Quite so. Massy doesn't work cheap but the result will be worth it. Is that all for now?"

"Yes. I thought I would join Barthélémy on site. Can you hold shop?" Barthélémy, his other associate, was working with the masons at the client's home.

Jerome nodded. "Go on. I have to fill in our ledger."

Reynaud rolled up his plan. "Will you join us for dinner to-night?"

"Maybe. Depends if I'm done. At the Montorgueil?"

"As always. See you there."

As soon as his associate was out the door, Jerome closed his eyes and rubbed his temples. Good Lord, he needed to get hold of himself. He'd barely slept last night, and now his nerves were on edge and his thoughts in a jumble. All day, the lines of his drawings had swum before his eyes, thwarting his attempts at tracing, altering and finalizing the simplest design. This was work that needed to be done, work that couldn't wait, and yet he'd given in to distraction.

Because of her. Stella. He couldn't stop thinking about the previous night. The baby's wails, the nurse with a candle in her hand, Stella's dark, determined gaze.

Yes, she'd told him he wasn't the father of the child. He hadn't any reason, nay, any *right* to discredit her. And he certainly hadn't any right to force himself into her life either, based on a tryst they'd had months ago.

He knew all of this. This was ration and reason speaking. Then why was guilt gnawing at him so? As if he should be doing all in his power to protect Stella and the baby from an unnamed threat, instead of trying to push them from his mind.

He hadn't been able to do the right thing before. To fix the consequences of his actions.

Leave her be! This isn't Annette's fault. You have no right to hurt her. Fight me if you must!

He pushed the memory back to the dark recesses of his mind. Fifteen years had passed, and Stella wasn't Annette. Yet the guilt simmered still, nagging him, sending prickles of discomfort in his stomach.

"Devil take it, man," he muttered to himself. "This must stop."

He opened the drawer to take out the heavy leather-bound ledger. Nothing like accounts to numb your brain against any semblance of human feeling. But before he could immerse himself in the rows of lines and columns, the bell of the front door tinkled.

Jerome rose from his chair to greet the client, an elegant gentleman with a lean figure, dark hair and large blue eyes, whose traits were all too familiar.

"Guy!" Jerome exclaimed. "*Seigneur,* what are you doing

here?"

They shook hands and Guy smiled. "Simply paying a visit to my dear brother-in-law."

At first Jerome had not been thrilled about Guy de Cazal marrying Antonia, given the rather precipitous nature of their relationship. In fact, there might have been a threat of pistols at dawn when he'd found out about it. But now, almost a year later, he had to admit their marriage was a happy one. From what Jerome—or anyone with eyes, really—could tell, Antonia was positively infatuated with her husband, and Guy always paid the utmost attention to her every need.

"Sit down, please," Jerome said, pulling out a chair. "When did you get to town?"

"Yesterday evening. I have business here to attend to, and I'd rather get it done quickly so I can go back to Antonia in Verneuil as soon as possible."

"I understand. The countryside is so much more agreeable than the capital during this season."

Guy's smile widened. "That's not the reason. You see, Antonia is with child."

Jerome blinked. Several times. His little sister, expecting? The same girl who held his hand while she was learning to walk, and pestered him to read her fairy tales, and blushed every time a stranger spoke to her?

Toinette. The family had called her that for years. But she was only Antonia now. Antonia de Cazal, who managed her own home and would soon be a mother.

"My heartfelt congratulations," he said. "This is excellent news. How is Antonia, then?"

"Ravenous," Guy simply replied.

"That's usually a good sign. Honorine was the same, and all her children came out stout and healthy."

"Oh, I'm most pleased about it. But it makes me miss home all the more."

Home. Yes, Guy and Antonia had a home. Honorine, her

husband and their children as well. Soon he'd have one more niece or nephew to hold.

His heart pinched painfully. In spite of his joy, the contrast with his own situation appeared to him all the more jarring. He was the eldest, and yet the sparsely furnished room where he slept above the shop was hardly what anyone would call a home.

"Are you all right?" Guy inquired.

"Yes. Just a bit tired is all. We have a lot of work on our hands, which I'm thankful for."

"Why don't we meet for dinner, then? You'll be at your leisure to tell me all about it."

He could tell Guy that he had already made plans to meet up with his associates. But at present he had no wish to discuss work. And maybe Guy could be trusted with what was plaguing him. After all, he was family. And though he was a loving husband and an ambitious, hard-working man, he certainly hadn't always led such an honorable life.

Guy wouldn't judge him, but neither would he simply brush off Jerome's concerns like Marbois might.

"Very well. Tell me where you're staying, and I'll come over when I'm finished."

Guy stood. "Wonderful. I know a few good places around the Palais Royal from when I lived here." He held his hands up. "Strictly food, I promise. No establishments of ill repute."

Jerome gave a dry laugh. "I'll hold you to it."

Though if he was being truthful, he might not have such a high moral ground to stand on. And Guy was about to find out as much.

Chapter Five

STELLA SIPPED A careful measure of wine, gaze darting over the guests present in Anatole Girard's salon. Men in colorful silk waistcoats and tight pantaloons, women in gauzy dresses cut low in front, their curls piled in extravagant chignons.

"Is this not a splendid fete, *madame*? Quite a crowd tonight. Girard's salons are always so amusing. Have you ever been to the folie he had built in Boulogne?"

The young man standing next to her had been trying to strike up a conversation for several minutes. The only reason Stella hadn't cut off his efforts was his relatively harmless air—skinny and sandy-haired with a collar and cravat that threatened to swallow him whole.

If she must attend Girard's salon tonight, she would rather whittle the evening away at the side of someone fastidious and dull rather than witty and dangerous.

"I'm afraid not, *monsieur*," she said succinctly. "I'm fairly new to the capital."

"Two months ago, he was kind enough to invite me so I might read some of my verses to his friends." The young man, who had introduced himself as Bastide Letourneur, attempted to puff out his chest. "And he was most generous with his praise. Good enough for Madame Bonaparte's salon, were his exact words."

She let him prattle on about his poetry, wondering when she might make her polite escape. Her gaze landed on Marcelline, who was on the arm of their portly host, greeting guests with the same aplomb as if she was Girard's wife and not his mistress. A gold chain with three sapphires glittered around her neck—Marcelline's asking price to be tied exclusively to him.

Who are you to judge? You were once the same. True, in the past she had on occasion accepted expensive gifts from suitors in exchange for warming their beds and acting the part of the adoring mistress, just like Mamma had taught her. Though it had always made Stella ill at ease to playact amorous passion off the stage, at least she was lucky enough that the gentlemen themselves hadn't been callous brutes.

Still, a part of her always had wondered what it would feel like not to have to act.

She knew now. But was none the better for it.

"Letourneur!" Girard turned towards them. "Shall we have you read tonight? Or are you too captivated by the beauty of your companion?"

"Your wish is my command, *monsieur*," Letourneur said, two spots of red appearing on his cheeks.

Girard shuffled over to them with Marcelline stepping lightly at his side. "I could not blame you. Madame Romano, you are ravishing indeed."

Stella forced herself to curl her lips into a demure smile and looked down at her fan. Anything too bold would no doubt attract Marcelline's ire.

"You are too kind, *monsieur*. Both for your compliment and your invitation."

Girard hooked his thumb in his waistcoat pocket and patted the side of his protuberant belly. "Now then, it is only natural. Marcelline insisted that your presence would enchant the gentlemen in attendance tonight, and that one of them might be lucky enough to obtain your favor."

Stella met Marcelline's gaze. Her smile was sweet, but her eyes were hard and cold as flint. That *stronza*. No need to wonder what this was all about. Marcelline was suspicious of her, and even more so that Stella wasn't actively seeking a protector. This was a test, nothing less.

Stella's first instinct had been to refuse Girard's invitation. But crossing Marcelline was a dangerous game, especially since Girard had invested part of his considerable fortune in venues such as the Olympique and other places of amusement.

Marcelline held all the cards, leaving Stella empty-handed. For now. Better to bide her time, then.

"There are but too many gentlemen to choose from in such a short amount of time," she replied in a playful tone. "Is love not a matter of endurance rather than haste?"

Girard laughed, and Marcelline along with him. "Very true, madame. You should join my party at the Beaujon Garden next week to further your inquiries."

Marcelline beamed at him. "The Beaujon Garden? Oh, what fun! The water show is simply to die for."

"They're inaugurating a new attraction called the Aerial Walks. A must-see, from what I've heard."

"In that case, Maria, you must absolutely come," Marcelline insisted.

Stella could only nod. Another night away from Clara, speaking to strangers whose acquaintance she had no desire to make. But what else could she do? This was for Clara's own good. A solid position within the troupe would bring in enough money to live comfortably for a while, even employ a second domestic to do the cleaning and the cooking to lighten Jane's burdens.

"It would be my pleasure, of course."

Later that evening, when she was finally alone in the fiacre bringing her home, Stella slumped back against the seat and closed her eyes. Maybe the Beaujon Garden would be entertaining at least and offer a temporary distraction from her troubles. When was the last time she had actually enjoyed herself at a party?

Signorina Cardinelli, won't you sing a song for us? What a treat it would be for my guests tonight!

Dio santo, every detail from that night was engraved in her mind, and it was all too easy to call up those memories now, as if they would wash away the tedium of Girard's salon.

She'd noticed Jerome as soon as he'd entered Imogen's ball-room. Not surprising, as he was a head taller than almost everyone else.

"He's the apprentice of Ludlow's architect," Imogen had whispered to her when she'd caught Stella looking. Staring, more like. "A Frenchman. But I'd be willing to bet he started out lifting stone and timber, with those arms."

By the time she'd indulged her hostess and sang an aria for the guests, Stella had gazed long enough at his muscular frame and brooding expression to decide that she must introduce herself to him.

Shocking behavior in polite society, but Imogen's parties were anything but polite. In fact, Imogen herself seemed to revel in the fact that the obscene wealth her late husband had left her made her impervious to scandal.

Besides, Stella had caught Jerome looking as well. And the way his gray eyes slid over the curves of her body made tendrils of heat bloom on her skin.

Impossible to ignore, or resist.

"I believe we have not met, sir. Are you a friend of Imo-gen's?"

He'd hesitated for a moment, as if surprised that she had addressed him directly, but then his expression had softened to courtesy. "Sadly not. I came here with one of my colleagues, who is well acquainted with her. Jerome Saint Yves."

"Stella Cardinelli. *Vous êtes français?*"

His smile was reserved but warm, and it made him even more handsome. "*Tout à fait, madame. Et vous êtes italienne, n'est-ce pas?*"

"Ah, so you heard my accent, then."

"More in French than in English, but it is beautiful just the same. And rare to meet someone who speaks both languages with such ease."

She'd sidled closer to him, barely keeping herself from running a hand up his chest to feel its hardness. "French is one of the languages of music. I would be a poor singer indeed if I did not hone my skills to master different tongues."

Later that night, when they were in bed together and Jerome had growled his pleasure as he took her again and again, he'd kept to English. It was only the next morning, at dawn, that he'd pulled her into a tight embrace and murmured a few words in French.

Tu es plus sublime que le soleil.

She'd kept those words and locked them safely away, only taking them out with great precaution when she was desperate for a burst of warmth and light.

She opened her eyes and looked out into the murky streets. Where was Jerome now? Was he lying with another woman, giving her pleasure? Telling her she was more sublime than the sun?

No, she refused to think about it. The vision alone… Vexing. *Infuriating.* But she couldn't help but hope these words had only been for her.

"HE SHOULD BE here any minute."

Guy and Jerome stopped at the end of the gallery which ran parallel to the gardens of the Palais Royal. The arcades provided welcome shade from the late afternoon sun, and at this hour, all manner of people, from wealthy bourgeois with golden pocket watches to modest employees in worn coats, were strolling along the long line of shops.

Jerome glanced nervously above his shoulder, and Guy

chuckled.

"Don't worry, the ladies of the night don't come out before sundown. If no one who sees you here, will assume the worst."

"That is not what worries me. I know you said you trusted this man with your life, but…"

But Jerome was not used to dealing with men like Guy's friend. From what Guy had told him when they'd dined together two days prior, Nicolas Lefevre made his money—and quite a lot of it—training savate fighters and setting up matches. He was also a frequent patron of the gaming hells of Palais Royal.

"If you want to find out who might be after your lady," Guy insisted, "there is no better man to ask than Nicolas. He has entries in the highest and lowest circles of Parisian society alike."

Heat crept onto Jerome's cheeks. "Stella Cardinelli isn't *my lady*," he muttered. "I am just… concerned for her welfare. Especially since she recently had a babe."

Raising an infant by herself, alone in the capital save for a nurse, working at the Olympique at the mercy of ill-intentioned rogues… How could he not be concerned? He could not simply stand by and leave her to whatever fate awaited. From a legal standpoint, as long as the babe wasn't his, he was under no obligation to help her, but he would be less than a man if he washed his hands of the entire situation.

"Pardon my presumption," Guy replied, a mischievous glint in his eyes, "though given the way you met…"

"Please, let us speak no more of it," Jerome said, his face burning hotter still. Bad enough that he'd had to reveal to his brother-in-law, a man he'd once accused of being a worthless rake, the reason why he was acquainted with Stella in the first place. "And not a word to Antonia."

"I would not want to worry her unnecessarily, given her delicate condition. Though I reckon you'd find her quite understanding on these matters."

Before Guy could elaborate, he glanced over Jerome's shoulder and waved. Jerome turned to find a tall gentleman heading in their direction. His blond curls were fashionably trimmed, and he was wearing a forest green double-breasted coat with matching breeches over a waistcoat of copper silk. With every long, easy stride he took, his silver-topped cane tapped on the pavement next to him, but a scar on his brow belied his elegant attire.

"Gentlemen," he said in a pleasant tone. "My apologies if I kept you waiting."

Guy glanced at his pocket watch. "Five minutes after the hour, that hardly warrants an apology. I know only too well that you are a busy man."

"Never too busy to meet with friends." He stopped and nodded to Jerome. "*Monsieur*. A pleasure to meet Madame de Cazal's brother."

"Likewise, *monsieur*," Jerome replied cautiously.

For now, he did not quite know what to make of this man. His clothes were extravagant, but his green eyes were sharp and intelligent. And though Lefevre was leaner than the laborers Jerome was used to working with, he knew a robust man when he saw one. Unsurprising, if he successfully trained savate fighters. Jerome had attended a boxing match back in London, but savate was reputed to be even quicker and more violent.

"Guy told me you might be in need of my assistance," Lefevre continued.

"Indeed."

Had Guy detailed the situation to him? Or should he explain the whole story all over again? But Lefevre simply smiled.

"I see you are a man of few words, Saint Yves. Rest assured, Guy has given me the long and short of your predicament. Shall we take a turn around the gardens?"

"You go on," Guy said. "I'm going to see if I can find some ribbons or dress trimmings to bring back to Antonia."

"Aren't you the lovelorn husband?" Lefevre teased. "Come then, Saint Yves, let us leave him to his shopping."

They strolled among the rows neatly lined with trees. Jerome cleared his throat. Guy may have told Lefevre about his circumstances, but he was going to have to ask the man for assistance himself.

"I'm grateful you agreed to meet me," he started. "How much has Guy told you exactly?"

"Enough. You're not the first man to have been bewitched by an opera singer, but it doesn't usually take such a dramatic turn. Your story is worth its own libretto."

"Believe me, I would rather skip right to the resolution," Jerome said darkly. "But I must make sure Stella is not in danger. Or at least, not in any more danger than she'd be as a woman of her profession."

Blast, the vision of that ruffian trying to break into her dressing room still made his blood simmer.

"And for that, you need my help," Nicolas stated.

Jerome nodded. "She's on the run from someone living in London—possibly a man she stole from, or who used to be her protector. He might be the father of her child as well."

"Do you have a name?"

It seemed almost too evident, but since he'd seen the seal on the diamond-encrusted box she'd sold Marbois, his thoughts kept dwelling on it. "Some popped-up English *aristo*, goes by Ludlow."

The very notion sent a sickly tremor through his stomach. His master had been hired by Ludlow along with other architects to renovate his London residence, and almost immediately rumors had started to circulate among the workers. Ludlow went above and beyond the usual licentiousness excepted from a nobleman. Mistresses and by-blows were one thing, but there were talks of bacchanals. Opium. Maids taken against their will and forced to service Ludlow's friends. One mason had sworn he knew of a girl who had taken her own life after what she'd endured. Ludlow's reputation was such that only young women in the direst of needs and without reference would agree to work for him.

Lefevre slowed his pace and stared ahead of him for a few moments, as if deep in thought. "An English lord, eh? He would need a long hand indeed to track her all the way to Paris."

"That bastard is richer than Croesus. I worked on the refurbishment of his house with the architect who trained me, and he owned a veritable mansion in Grosvenor Street."

"It's not just a question of money," Lefevre said. "If he wanted to send some thugs after the lady, he would have to be dealing in dubious business from across the Channel and know the right people to ask."

"Would you know who to ask?"

Once again, Lefevre simply smiled. "You said you needed my help. Is that not why I'm here?"

Chapter Six

Meet at the pavilion of Beaujon Garden, tomorrow night at sundown. – NL

A SKINNY BOY delivered the message to Jerome outside his shop. No explanation, just a time and place. And here he was, after paying a few francs to enter, in the middle of a colorful crowd of revelers, craning his neck for a glimpse of Lefevre's fair hair and tall frame.

He'd heard much about the pleasure gardens of Paris and the variety of entertainment one could find there—magic lanterns, water shows, pantomimes—but had never experienced it for himself. Richly attired or modestly dressed, the people mixed in a raucous brouhaha, as if they were not done celebrating this new era of freedom and gaiety after years of bloodshed and deprivation.

A sudden urge to join in seized him. After all, he could certainly sympathize with that feeling. Everywhere he looked, there was a siren call to let loose and enjoy himself. The wine merchants peddling bottles, the couples twirling to a waltz on a wooden dais, the women clad in flimsy linen gowns, walking arm in arm, their lips painted red and their hair in loose chignons.

Take what you want and don't worry about tomorrow. He closed his eyes and inhaled, seeking countenance. No, he wouldn't give in. That wasn't the sort of man he was. But it was getting more and more difficult to keep the yearning at bay. He had kept it tightly locked up ever since returning from London, but God help him, seeing Stella again had reminded him that it was still alive and well, biding its time.

Waiting for him to slip up, just once, so it could take over again and do away with decency.

A mop of blond curls under a dark silk hat caught his eyes. Ah, there was Lefevre at last, without his cane though just as garishly dressed, with a mustard waistcoat and a bright crimson jacket. And a relief it was to be distracted from his previous line of thought.

"How do you fare, Saint Yves?" Lefevre asked in a jaunty tone. "First time at Beaujon?"

Jerome nodded. "I am not usually for such crowded places."

"I take it you didn't go to Vauxhall in London, then."

"That was more a question of not having much money to spend on entertainment. Or anything beyond necessities."

Lefevre's expression didn't falter, but his eyes took on a steely quality. "Yes, Guy told me all about the hardships of exile, though he only had his mother to care for."

And what had Lefevre done during the Revolution to survive? His name didn't indicate aristocratic antecedents, but Lord knew the nobility hadn't been the Widow's only victims. Now wasn't the time to inquire, though. Maybe he should ask Guy next time he was in town.

"Standing here, all of that seems very far away," Jerome simply said. "Almost like a nightmare we've all woken from."

Lefevre grinned. "Yes, and the good people of Paris are awake and ravenous for fun. Which is why I asked you here this evening. Come along."

He followed Lefevre through the crowd to a towering construction. A steep incline fitted with what looked like a wagonway led up to a small pavilion, ten meters from the ground, and two other slopes led away from it in a precipitous curve. A throng of people were already queuing at the side entrances.

"The Aerial Walks are being inaugurated," Nicolas said. "Quite impressive, wouldn't you say?"

Jerome could only stare in awe. A feat of architecture, certainly, but the idea of riding a wagon up that slope was enough to make his stomach lurch—let alone the return trip. "I've never seen anything like it."

"Neither has anyone else. The idea came from the Russian court, if you can believe it. Anyone who's anyone in the Parisian *beau monde* will be here tonight to see it work. With a bit of luck, your lady will turn up."

Jerome tore his eyes away from the construction. "What makes you think that?"

"She's a singer at the Olympique, is she not? Many gentlemen love nothing more than to parade around with a woman like her at their arm, especially at this sort of event."

Blast. He was right. And if Jerome laid eyes on some foppish fool with Stella on his arm... He shook the loathsome image away. No time to lose his temper when he wasn't even sure how the evening would unfold.

"If she does show, I'm not sure how that would help my case. Did you start inquiring into who might be after her?"

"I have a few leads, but it's going to take a bit of time to follow through," Lefevre replied. "In any case, the important thing is to let anyone with ill intentions know she's got a... sturdy ally on her side." He observed Jerome closely. "Did you ever consider learning savate?"

"Maybe later," Jerome grunted. "How am I supposed to spot her in this damned crowd?"

"I'll help you keep an eye out," Lefevre added. "What does she look like?"

Heaven. The word came to his mind, but he kept it from passing his lips. Heaven that could send a man straight to hell, more like, with those sumptuous curves and exquisite smile. But he would have to stick to the facts to answer Lefevre, lest he come off as a lust-stricken fool.

"Black hair, thick and curly. Dark eyes. Pale skin. Very pale, in fact. Quite a remarkable contrast with her hair. She's about this tall—" He tapped his shoulder with the edge of his hand. "—and plump, but with rather a small waist. Not at all the willowy figure that's the fashion. Nevertheless, she moves with more elegance and grace than most women. Carries herself like a queen, one might say."

There, that ought to do it. Lefevre nodded, his lips quivering. "A very precise description indeed. Let us stay on this side so we can see the people coming in."

For a long while, they stood together, idly discussing the latest roadworks near the Louvre and Guy's recent investments in the horse trade while they watched more people filter in. Many men had a flask in hand, and Jerome half expected Lefevre to produce his own, just like Marbois always did, but none came.

"You do not drink, *monsieur?*" Jerome asked.

Lefevre shook his head. "Never when there are thugs and thieves abound. I've seen at least four people getting their pockets picked since we got here."

Ah. He had better pay closer mind then. Yet a loud clatter diverted his attention. Two small wagons, large enough to fit in one person each, ascended to the top of the slope to the clanking of chains and the cheers of the onlookers. What sort of hidden mechanism hauled the two wagons to the apex? His mind whirled with the possibilities. Some type of cable and pulley system? Once the wagons arrived at the top, they were separated and set loose on the two curved slopes, launching the passengers at breakneck speed. Nobody could pay him enough to embark on the contraption himself, but he'd willingly part with his purse for a look at the construction plans.

"See here, Saint Yves, I spotted someone who fits your description."

Jerome turned back to the crowd and followed Lefevre's gaze.

Yes. By God, it was unmistakably her. Wearing a blue linen dress, a silvery shawl thrown about her shoulders. She was walking with a group of seven or so, and at her arm was a red-cheeked, wide-eyed young man.

"That's Stella," he said.

"Who's that she's with? Surely not a protector. He looks like he's too young to grow a proper mustache."

"I have no idea." And damn, if he didn't want to find out.

Stella glanced in their direction, as if she'd somehow felt someone watching her from afar. Their eyes met. She stopped. And frowned.

Then turned to her companion to excuse herself, and marched in their direction.

"Blast," Jerome muttered. "Were we supposed to try and follow her from afar?"

Lefevre clapped his back. "That sort of thing never works, if it makes you feel any better."

Jerome braced himself. To say Stella looked displeased to see him was an understatement. Her eyes were fairly burning with anger.

She stopped in front of them and lifted her chin to glare at him. "*Monsieur*. What a strange coincidence to run into you tonight."

"*Madame*," he replied evenly. "Not much of a coincidence, since apparently half the city came out in celebration of the Aerial Walks."

Her gaze snapped to Lefevre. "And I see you came with another of your friends. One can only hope he is less of a cad."

"Nicolas Lefevre," he said, all courtesy. "A pleasure."

"Well, Monsieur Lefevre, I would like to have a discussion with Monsieur Saint Yves in private, if you don't mind."

Jerome raised his eyebrows. "Private? Hardly the time and place for it. Besides, it seems as though you have a gentleman waiting for you."

A low blow, but by God, seeing her with another man, puny though he may be, had set his blood boiling.

"*Now*," Stella growled. "And we shall see if you are man enough to tell me face to face the reason of your presence here."

STELLA GLANCED OVER her shoulder as she led Jerome further away from the crowd. Letourneur and the rest of Girard's group were moving over to the side entrances of the Aerial Walks. *Porca miseria*, she needed to hurry if she wanted to catch up with them without rousing Marcelline's suspicions, or else this whole evening would be in vain. But this could not wait another moment.

Beneath a row of trees leading further into the gardens, she whipped around to face Jerome.

"Out with it then," she demanded. "Did you or did you not come here with the intention of spying on me?"

He glowered, his gray eyes a storm. Was he contemplating a lie? Finally, he let out a deep breath.

"Spying on you requires discretion, of which I am apparently incapable. But since the rest of society is here, I did hope to run across you, yes. I cannot simply leave you in this precarious situation without trying to help."

"Why not?" she retorted. "Why can't you? We are... We are nothing to each other."

She regretted the words as soon as they passed her lips. *She* was the liar. What had happened between them, fleeting though it may have been, was far from nothing. At least for her. And maybe for Jerome as well. Had he also been dreaming about that night for months on end? Or was it really just duty speaking?

His gaze hardened to flint. "We may be nothing, *madame*, but I will not stand by while you risk harm."

The presumption of this man was too much to bear. Had she not made the voyage all the way from London by herself and managed to keep Clara safe?

She poked his chest with her finger. "Listen here, I have been looking after myself for quite some time. I do not need anyone to tell me how to best behave. Now, if you'll excuse me, I must rejoin my party."

Jerome narrowed his eyes. "Are you going to take a turn on the Aerial Walks? Your paltry companion will fly out of the wagon, if it doesn't topple over and plummet to the ground first."

She raised an eyebrow. "You think it's dangerous?"

"No. I just choose to believe it is until proven otherwise by a comprehensive study of its design. How did they make sure that the wagon doesn't build up too much speed to properly stay on the tracks through the curve?"

Her anger melted a little. Jerome was the only man she had ever met who spoke with such perspicacity and attention for detail. The night they'd met, he'd commented on the particular stucco decorations of Imogen's ceiling, seemingly unaware of how bizarre it was for a gentleman to engage in that sort of conversation when the lady had already made her intentions clear. And she had made them very clear indeed.

"Fine," she replied, grasping at the remains of her initial ire. "You can watch while I test its soundness. We shall see if you're right."

A muscle clenched his neck. "Stella…"

Oh, to hear him say her name again… She must go now and keep her resolve intact. "Do not follow me."

And with that, she turned away and hurried off to the side entrance, where she spotted Letourneur waving at her.

"Over here, *madame*," he called out. "I thought you'd lost your way in the crowd. Come, the queue is moving forward rather quickly."

She forced a weak smile. Only then did she dare to glace back and see if Jerome had complied with her demand.

Her blood froze. He had indeed stayed back near the trees, but two burly men, red-faced with drink, were advancing on him. One of them pushed him squarely in the chest. Jerome raised his fist, but before he could land a blow, the other grabbed his arm and pinned it behind him.

What in the devil? Where on earth had the attackers come from?

"Madame Romano? Are you coming?"

Blast. She couldn't simply let two ruffians beat Jerome to prove a point. But what could she do?

That other man. Nicolas Lefevre. Where had he gone? If only she could find him…

"Madame Romano!" Letourneur craned his neck to follow her gaze. "I say, what's happening over there? A couple of drunkards brawling?"

A couple of people had turned to look now, but none of them moved a centimeter. Devil take them all, it was just another form of entertainment to them. She shook her head helplessly at Letourneur. "Go on without me, *monsieur*. Pray forgive me."

She dashed back the way she'd come. Certainly, Lefevre couldn't have gone far. She weaved through the crowd, heart pounding, gaze darting to and fro. Finally, she spotted him talking with a smartly dressed couple.

"Monsieur Lefevre," she called.

He turned and frowned. "Madame?"

"Quickly, Jerome needs you."

Lefevre bounded after her. She pointed toward the fight, which had moved further into the shadows of the tree-lined path.

Jerome struggled with one opponent, while the other leaned over and spit blood on the ground. Lefevre ran straight into the fray. His arm snaked around the neck of Jerome's assailant. With a sharp jerk, his knee landed in the small of the ruffian's back. The man roared with pain and slumped to his knees.

Jerome dodged the pair and hauled the second man up by his lapels. A single punch to his jaw sent his body flying in an arc to land on the dusty path.

Stella covered her mouth to stifle a gasp. They were fighting two against two now. Nicolas rained well-aimed jabs on his man. Jerome dodged just in time to avoid another fist to the jaw but replied with a single powerful blow. His assailant hit the ground again.

A crowd gathered as if to enjoy an improvised boxing match, yelling encouragement to the fighters. And cheering, actually *cheering*, when the two ruffians finally fell back and lurched into the trees.

Lefevre and Jerome staggered back to her, breathless, and her gaze settled on a bloody bruise on Jerome's lip.

"*Dio santo*, what on earth happened?" she exclaimed. "I leave you for a moment and turn to see you brawling with these brutes!"

Jerome gave a dry laugh. "One of them claimed I'd looked at him funny. Ape-drunk but strong as an ox, the bastard."

"Did they want to rob you?"

Lefevre shrugged. "Unlikely. Some men come here looking for a fight the same way others come looking for a quick tryst in the hedge maze. See, Saint Yves, this should convince you to let me teach you savate."

"Without your help, I might have ended up with worse than a cut lip," Jerome said. "And without yours, *madame*, Lefevre would not have come to my aid so quickly."

Their gazes met and held for a moment. Stella fished in her reticule for her handkerchief and raised it to his mouth, meaning to press it against the bruise. No, too bold. She let her hand fall away and handed it to him.

"Here, to staunch the blood," she said. "It's clean. Freshly laundered and pressed."

Jerome nodded. "Thank you. It seems you're the one who kept me from harm tonight. I suppose that makes us even."

Even, yes. Though that meant they truly had no further reason to see each other now.

"Right, then it is time for me to go home," she said.

By all means, she should try and rejoin Girard's party. But the very idea of making nice with Letourneur while facing Marcelline's pointed questions and thinly veiled insults exhausted her. If she had to keep up this grotesque charade, perhaps it could wait until tomorrow.

"Without trying the Aerial Walks?" Lefevre asked.

"I've had enough adventure for one evening. Goodnight, *messieurs.*"

An hour later, as the fiacre pulled to a halt in front of her boarding house, she glanced at her reticule on the seat. She'd let Jerome keep her handkerchief. It was silly, really. He would probably discard it without a thought. But what if he sought to return it? Was that what she desired, deep down?

She shook her head and exited the fiacre. What she needed was a good night's sleep to clear her mind of all this nonsense.

As she reached the landing, the door to her flat swung open, and Jane's head appeared. Her hair straggled beneath her mob cap. Tears stained her face.

God almighty. *Clara.* Had something happened to Clara?

"There ye are, miss, at last," Jane cried. "I heard ye coming up the stairs. Lud help us, whatever will we do now?"

Chapter Seven

THE FIRST THING he saw when he opened his eyes was the handkerchief, stark white against the dark wood of his nightstand.

Jerome blinked sleepily then stared at it for several long moments. Delicate lace lined the edge, an S entwined with a C finely stitched in one corner in white thread.

After Stella's hasty retreat from the Beaujon Garden, he'd pressed his cuff to his lip instead of sullying the spotless white. He cared little for his clothes beyond functionality.

But *this*. This piece of her, so pristine and exquisite, he didn't have the heart to stain.

He reached for the scrap of linen and inhaled its scent, as he had the evening before. Jasmine. Like her hair. Soft, thick curls he could bury his face in, stroke, grab by the handful…

He rolled to his back with a groan, the sheets sliding over his heated skin. Devil take it, he was hard. Painfully so. He'd tried, he had. But crushing lust held him in a vise-grip, drumming through his veins until it blotted out reason.

By God, when he'd come to her straight from the fight, his breath still short and his blood still pounding, the way she'd held his gaze… Angry at him, of course, but something other than fury had simmered in her dark eyes.

There was no escaping it. A single look from Stella, sidelong and penetrating, set him ablaze, and the hungry beast within clawed at him relentlessly, demanding to be let out and fed. He must relieve some of the strain. Loathe as he was to give in to his baser impulses, it was better this way, when he knew there would be no consequence but for his own pride.

He wrapped his right hand around his length, keeping the handkerchief in his left hand, losing himself in the vivid, flowery scent. A vision from their night of passion immediately swirled to the surface of his mind, as if it had been lying in wait. Stella, her back arched and her head thrown back, that mane of dark hair tumbling down her back. Straddling him. Lowering herself onto him, gripping his cock in her tight, wet heat, a breathy moan escaping from her parted lips.

His fingers moved up and down, up and down. Again, and again, and again, she'd rolled her hips in a maddening way while he ran his hands up her creamy thighs, up the curve of her waist, to cup her quivering breasts and squeeze the berry-red tips…Then she'd leaned forward and grasped his wrists and led them back to her waist. Handing control over to him, her eyes glazed with lust.

More. Give me more, I beg you.

The movements of his hand quickened. Roughened. He'd pinned her down as he thrust up inside of her, and slapped the side of her thigh, eliciting a louder moan…

He inhaled deeply. Jasmine. Stella's skin. *Their* skin, sliding together, and he pounded harder and harder and…

His eyes slammed shut. The burning tightness snapped low in his belly, and spilled over in a long spurt on his hand and stomach. For several seconds he let himself catch his breath, the images slowly receding, the hunger momentarily satiated.

Only to be replaced by gnawing guilt. He sat up abruptly and wiped himself with the sheet. True, this was not the first time he had surrendered and let memories of his night with Stella bring him to climax. But it was one thing to give himself over when he thought he would never see her again, and quite another to do so now. Stella was here. She was in danger. And he was trying to protect her.

And he'd just let his raging lust obliterate every single thought in his head.

He swung his legs to the side of his bed and carefully returned the handkerchief to the nightstand. Enough. Thankfully, work awaited downstairs, quite enough to force his mind into more productive avenues.

He washed and dressed hastily, then trudged down to the shop. Barthélémy and Reynaud were already leaning over one of the drawing tables, scribbling measurements.

"Not like you to sleep in," Barthélémy joked, his eyes still on the plan. "We thought you'd taken ill."

An illness might be preferable than to be plagued with these appetites. "Not ill. Just had an eventful night."

His associates both glanced up and took in his bruised lip. "*Seigneur*," Reynaud exclaimed. "What the devil happened to you, man?"

"Some drunkards at Beaujon Garden decided they wanted a brawl."

Barthélémy raised an eyebrow. "Never pictured you as the sort to go to a pleasure garden. Did you make a night of it? I hear Beaujon doesn't empty until dawn."

"Hardly. I still have enough sense to sleep."

After Stella had left, he'd bid his own adieu to Lefevre and had walked home. Not that it had helped to clear his mind or cool his blood.

And he'd held that damned handkerchief tightly between his fingers the entire way. The way he'd held it to his nose just now.

Damn and blast.

"Well, a messenger boy was waiting for you when we got here." Reynaud pulled a small letter from his pocket and handed it to him. "Said it was urgent."

Jerome snatched the letter and opened it. His gaze darted

over the graceful, slanted writing. And his throat tightened more with each word.

Dear Jerome, a pressing matter has come up. Please come at your earliest convenience. 43 Gramont Street. Stella.

Good Lord, what had happened? It must be grave indeed if she was asking him for assistance. There wasn't a moment to lose.

"I must attend to this right away," he rasped.

Reynaud frowned. "Now? Marbois is waiting on the updated plans. You said yourself we should have him look them over no later than tomorrow."

"This cannot wait either," he retorted.

He wanted to add that it wouldn't take long, but he had not the faintest idea what Stella needed of him. His only conviction was that he would do whatever it took to help her.

⇒⟩⟩⟩⟨⟨⟨⇐

"Speak slowly now and tell me everything that happened."

Stella held Clara in her arms, bouncing her on her knees and dangling a tassel of brightly colored ribbons in front of her. She glanced at Jane next to her, then at Jerome who sat on the chair opposite the divan. His gray eyes intent on Jane and his jaw clenched.

"I was sewing, right 'ere on this couch, and Clara was sleeping like an angel, when I 'eard someone bang on the door. Three times—*boom boom boom*. I didn't say nothing, I just waited. And then more bangin'—*boom boom boom*. I can still 'ear it now."

Jane sniffled and wrapped her skinny arms around herself. "I didn't know what to do. Miss Cardinelli was not gone an hour. So I went to the door and asked who it was. A man answered in French, I couldn't understand 'im, then another one, in English this time. And 'e said... 'e said..."

She sniffled again, and Stella reached out to squeeze her shoulder. "Go on, Jane. It's all right."

"'E said to open up or 'e'd break the door down 'imself to get to the—pardon me for saying—lying thieving slut who lived 'ere."

Jerome's fists tightened on his lap. "Did he have an accent?"

"I couldn't say, sir. I was in a panic. I screamed at 'em to leave, and Clara started to cry in her crib, poor dear. But then I 'eard some neighbors come out into the staircase and that big man who lives right upstairs with his family, 'e told 'em to clear off and that 'e had a pistol loaded and ready. And then they left."

"I asked our neighbor this morning if he'd gotten a look at those brutes," Stella said, "but the staircase was dark and nothing stood out to him."

Jerome nodded, gaze closed in as if deep in thought. Then he addressed Jane again. "Thank you for telling me this. I promise I will try and assist you as best I can so you are not terrorized by such criminals again."

"May God hear ye, sir," she replied. "Shall I take Clara now, miss? It'll soon be time to feed 'er."

"Of course."

Stella kissed the top of Clara's head, then handed her to Jane, who retreated to her room. Jerome sighed deeply. For a moment, she simply drank in the sight of him, letting his presence soothe her. As if the simple fact of his presence might dissuade wrongdo-ers from knocking at her door again.

If only it were that simple.

"It doesn't make sense," he said finally. "Why make enough noise to wake the dead when they could have simply picked the lock and entered?"

"Please, don't say that, it makes me sick even to contemplate it," Stella replied weakly.

"There must be a reason," Jerome insisted. "Maybe they're trying to intimidate you—they or rather whoever sent them."

Stella crossed her arms in front of her chest. "Well, they've made an excellent job of it. We cannot stay here another night. I would not be able to sleep, much less leave Jane and Clara alone whilst I go to the opera."

He blinked. "You're performing tonight?"

Dio santo, the very idea of getting up on stage made her stomach lurch, but she had no choice. "I am owed my first wages. If I don't go, I will not be paid. And we need the money if we are to leave Paris."

Jerome bolted to his feet. "Leave Paris? Is that your plan?"

"What else can we do? We cannot possibly stay here if we are being hunted down."

Though Ludlow no doubt had the means to keep chasing her, and it was certainly him behind all of this. Somehow, he'd managed to trace her.

Lying, thieving slut.

Cold dread sank into her bones.

"He's letting me know he found me," she said, voicing her thoughts aloud. "He wants me to be afraid."

Jerome's eyes narrowed. "Who is *he*?"

She looked down at her hands. "The Marquess of Ludlow. This should come as no surprise to you. You saw that box, and you know how much it was worth."

Though he didn't know the rest of the story. How long could she keep it from him?

Jerome nodded once and sat back down. "Indeed. But have you considered that you leaving Paris is precisely what he wants?"

"How so?"

"If he's got his men watching you, he knows it will be easier to strike while you're on the road, alone with Jane and Clara. Rather than here, in a crowded city where you have some connections at least."

"Connections?" Stella huffed. "You mean Marcelline? Girard and his ilk? Should I simply take a protector and hope the door he provides me is sturdy?"

Jerome's gaze darkened. "Not a protector, no. Such a man

might dismiss you at the first sign of trouble, and besides, the babe should be protected as well."

She pressed her lips together. "Of that I am all too aware, believe me."

"What you need is someone who will be bound to you and Clara in the eyes of the law and society at large. Someone whose protection will be constant and unfailing, night and day."

She frowned. "Forgive me, but it sounds as if you are describing a husband."

Jerome sat perfectly still, his gaze unflinching. "I am. And if you are willing, I am ready to fill that position myself."

Chapter Eight

F OR A MOMENT, Stella could only stare at Jerome in shock. She could not have been more astonished if he had suddenly grown another head.

"You… You are offering marriage?" she finally managed. "Are you mad?"

Jerome's gaze darkened. "Why would I be mad to make such an offer?"

A man like him, with a respectable profession and an honorable name, binding himself to a woman like her, an opera singer who had already been the mistress of other men… A preposterous notion. Jerome would be barred from polite society forever. And while he had never mentioned his family, surely any living relative of his would be scandalized at the match. How could he not see it?

She shook her head. "Think of the risk, your standing, your name."

"I risk far less than you in this situation."

"You work as an architect, do you not? Prospective clients will shun you."

He shrugged his shoulders. "If my future clients are anything like Marbois, I very much doubt they will give a fig about who I choose to wed."

"Your family then," she insisted. "Have you no relatives who would condemn this marriage?"

A flicker of doubt passed through his gray eyes. "Explaining this to my sisters might be a bit complicated, yes. But I do not stand to be disinherited, if that is what you mean. Both my parents died long ago."

She studied him in silence. His fluency in English had led her to guess he was one of the many French immigrants who had fled the Terror years before. He'd only mentioned it was his last night in London. And indeed, he had left early the next morning to return to his homeland for the first time in a decade.

But she was left to imagine whether any of his loved ones had gone to the guillotine or been swept away in a mindless massacre. Whether he was alone in the world. Whether he had sweetheart waiting for him on the other side of the Channel.

Now he was revealing bits and pieces of his life. Deceased parents. *Sisters.* Certainly, he would not risk ruining *their* reputation.

"Tell me at least that your sisters are…"

"Married. Yes. I would never do anything that would harm their social standing." He tapped his fingers on the armrest. "At worst this would result in a very uncomfortable conversation. But if I tell them Clara is mine…"

Stella's eyes widened. Jerome, lie to give Clara the Saint Yves name? And *she* would have to take his name as well. In the eyes of the law, he would hold sway over them both. Her throat tightened.

"You would claim her as yours."

"That would be the point, would it not?"

She rose from the divan. It was as if the walls of the room were closing in on her. She needed air. Needed to get away, but there was nowhere to go. She paced around the room, arms crossed in front of her. "Explain, then. Explain your reasoning, for I am not yet convinced this isn't utter lunacy."

He leaned forward, his eyes never leaving her. "If we marry,

Ludlow will know that you are not without support or allies, that he cannot simply attack you without risking retaliation. You would no longer have to hide behind a false identity, and you would have legitimate status as my wife. Not to mention financial security."

"I have always earned my own wages, and I continue to do so today," she retorted.

"And how will you fare if you are forced to flee Paris? How will you earn a living then?"

Devil take him, did he think she did not know how precarious her situation was? But to put her fate, and Clara's, in the hands of a man... No matter if Jerome was unlike any other she'd met before.

Loyal. Resilient. Unselfish.

Dio santo, could she really accept?

"Most importantly," he continued, "Clara would also benefit from the protection of my name. Her father has not recognized her, has he?"

She stopped, facing away from him. "No."

"Is it Ludlow?"

Her heart thudded painfully in her chest. "Yes."

She turned. His mouth was pressed in a tight line, his gray eyes blazing.

"Then I am even less surprised that he has shirked his responsibility, given his reputation." He sniffed. "All too often those who heed their impulses and neglect their duty leave others to deal with the consequences."

It was easy to guess what was going through his mind. He had put those pieces of the puzzle he had together, and drawn the conclusion that she had stolen a priceless heirloom from her former protector and fled with his bastard child. For she had not lied to him, but neither had she corrected him in the assumption that she was Clara's mother.

She should tell him now. Tell him that Ludlow had never laid a hand on her, though not for lack of trying. The very idea was so repulsive that no amount of lavish gifts had ever managed to sway her.

What difference would it make? Probably none. But even a responsible, dutiful man might not go so far as taking in the child of two perfect strangers, one of whom was dead and the other dangerous.

If there was the slightest chance Jerome might rescind his offer…

On the horizon, another future beckoned. Relief. Stability. At least for a time. It shone like a jewel, just out of her reach, taunting her.

She might grab it. She might fall short. But she had to try. It was either that, or be thrown onto the road again, not knowing where she would land. She had to do it for Clara. No matter if Jerome believed she had lain with that wretch.

"Are you truly ready to deal with those consequences yourself?" she asked in a quiet voice.

His gaze cleared, and his mouth softened. "I wouldn't have offered if I wasn't."

She took a deep breath. "Very well, then. I accept your offer."

He stood and gave a short nod. "Good. I am… pleased to be able to assist you in this manner. I will arrange for a civil ceremony and find new lodgings for you. For us." A slight flush dotted his cheeks. "In the meantime, you can all stay in my room above the shop. Cramped quarters for two women and a babe, but at least you can rest easy. I will be right downstairs."

"But where will you sleep?"

He waved his hand. "There's a bench in my study. I will make do with a cover and some pillows. Believe me, I managed to sleep in far worse conditions when we were making the trip to London."

Stella stepped closer to him. "And after we are married?"

Married. This tall, broad-shouldered man would be her husband, and she his wife. In name only, or would he expect them to share a bed?

There would be nothing to hinder his desires now. No concern for honor or decency. By rights, she would be his. But this time the notion did not unsettle her, and trepidation of a different sort made her nerves hum.

He stood straight as a rod, hands clasped behind his back, his gaze evading hers. "Rest assured, I will not impose anything on you against your wishes." Then, as if remembering something, he dug into his pocket and took out her handkerchief. "Here. It's clean. I didn't want to get blood on it."

"You could have kept it," she replied. "I have others."

The flush on his cheeks deepened. "It's better if you take it back."

She pressed the fine linen between her fingers. Perhaps she was letting her own desires cloud her reason and imagining that he yearned for the same thing. Or perhaps not. She would simply have to further her inquiries on their wedding night.

GRUNTS AND SHOUTS rang out clear as day from inside the small church. Jerome paused for a moment and inspected the dilapidated building. Yes, this was the place Lefevre had told him about, right before they parted at Beaujon Garden.

"If you need to find me, I'm at Saint Aphrodise most mornings. Follow the alley off Tonneliers Street, north of the Palais Royal."

The church must have been a beauty before the Revolution. Solid stone blocks formed thick walls supported by sturdy romanesque arches, and the tympanum above the portal curved in perfect proportion to the rest of the structure. But the intricate sculptures of saints had been defaced, their heads crudely chopped off, and black traces of fires marred the white facade. The wooden doors were broken down, the stain glasses reduced to mere shards. Jerome shook his head. A shame.

Inside, the empty nave stretched toward the space for the altar, cleared of pews and sacred ornaments. A makeshift ring delimited with ropes stood in the center. Two young men, bare but for their breeches, exchanged volleys of quick, brutal punches and kicks, while a few others urged them on from the sidelines.

Lefevre stood at a corner of the ring, monitoring the bout, his face a mask of concentration.

"That's it, Matthieu. He's weaker on the right. Strike now! Goddamn you, Emeric, use your feet."

One of the fighters took a heavy punch to the side and fell to his knees. Good Lord, was this the sport Lefevre had offered to teach him? It hurt just to watch the fight. Lefevre clapped his hands three times and the men stopped, breathless and slick with sweat.

Jerome stood at the base of a pillar. Better not bother Lefevre while he was busy with his pupils. But when Lefevre spotted him, he simply smiled and waved him over, as if they were meeting at a tavern.

"Good to see you, Saint Yves. Funny but I was going to drop by your shop later today. I've got news that might interest you."

Jerome took off his hat and rubbed the side of his head. "So have I."

"Take a seat, then," Lefevre said, motioning him towards a wooden bench. "The boys can practice without me for a bit."

Once Jerome had told him about the ruffians who had shown up at Stella's door and his offer to marry her, Lefevre sighed and pulled a flask from the pocket of his trousers.

"I don't suppose congratulations are in order, but let us toast to your engagement nonetheless. *Santé!*"

Lefevre took a swig, and Jerome crinkled his brow. "I thought you didn't drink."

"I said I don't drink among criminals. But here—" He spread his arms wide and looked to the ring, where another fight had started. "—I am among friends."

Jerome took the flask from him and drank. The alcohol

bloomed on his tongue in a fire of herbal aromas. "Chartreuse?"

"I find it more invigorating than cognac. Now, what is your next move?"

By God, he hardly knew where to begin. "Ask Marbois for an advance on my salary so I can pay for new lodgings and hire help. Or maybe inquire on what would be available first. Yes, that would be the most urgent. No, wait, I must arrange for a civil ceremony above all else."

Not to mention write to his sisters to explain that an encounter in London with a young lady had resulted in a babe, and that he must do the honorable thing and marry her. After all the sermons on proper behavior he'd delivered over the years, he was dreading it almost as much as having to deal with Ludlow and his henchmen.

"I can help you with the lodgings," Lefevre said. "A lady of my acquaintance is always the first to learn when a place has been vacated in the area, or even when it's about to be."

"How so?"

"She takes in laundry. Believe me, these women know everyone's business, rich or poor. There's no hiding anything from them."

Jerome tried not to think about what he'd used his sheet for only two days past. "Right. If it's not too much trouble, I gladly accept. Nothing too extravagant, but clean and spacious, large enough for a family of three and two maids."

A family. All his life, he had strived to take up his father's mantle. Evrard Saint Yves had been a family man, first and foremost. And now Jerome himself was stepping into this role, he couldn't help but feel woefully unprepared. How the devil would he manage? Acting as head of the family when his two sisters were grown wasn't the same as having a wife and child under his responsibility. Especially when said wife was a walking, breathing temptation combined with a fiery temper and a will of iron.

It would be like trying to reign in a storm. And reigning in the storm within him as well. For he would be damned if he treated

Stella with anything less than the utmost courtesy, after what she'd been through.

"Noted." Lefevre leaned closer. "As for the two dogs who came barking at your fiancée's door, I have a lead. There's an Englishman hiring hands to do some dirty work in the city."

"Ludlow?"

Simply saying the man's name, picturing him touching Stella… His vision clouded with red. How desperate must have she been to accept Ludlow's attentions? Unless he'd forced himself on her. By God, what he wouldn't give for a few rounds in that ring with the bastard, no matter if his form was lacking.

"Not Ludlow, no," Lefevre replied, pulling him out of his thoughts. "A smuggler who operates a ring between Paris and the Channel. Goes by the name of the Kingfisher. I found one of his men and had a little chat with him last night. It seems he's a lover of Mozart, because he was at the Olympique the night Stella debuted in *The Marriage of Figaro*."

"Devil take him," Jerome growled. "I hope you gave him the beating he deserved."

Lefevre grinned. "I might have smacked him around a bit, yes, but he offered up what I wanted quickly enough. Confirmation that he was hired specifically to give Stella a good scare."

"Did he say why?"

"These brutes aren't paid to ask questions. And in the grand scheme of things, they're a small catch indeed. But now that the bird knows we're on his trail, he might take some time to lie low and regroup."

Jerome nodded. "Let us hope so. I want Stella to feel safe, for as long as possible."

Lefevre took his flask back and raised it again. "Might as well enjoy the honeymoon, eh?"

Jerome sighed. That was another matter he would have to take in hand, and just as likely to make him lose sleep.

Chapter Nine

"**D**O YOU LIKE it?"

Jerome watched Stella as she took in her surroundings. She was wearing a dove gray dress with a rose sash, her hair swept up in a simple chignon. A tendril had escaped the pins and curled on the nape of her neck. His fingers tickled with the urge to take the silky lock between his fingers and tuck it back in the chignon.

"Yes. It's beautiful."

Beautiful. His gaze swept over the front hall of the house he had rented in Castellane Street. For once, he didn't linger on the details or study how balanced the proportions were, and slid right back to Stella instead.

Ever since she emerged from the shop that afternoon to take the fiacre to the town hall, he could scarcely take his eyes off her. Her attire was plain compared to the night they'd met and a far cry from what she wore on stage, but somehow she was even lovelier than usual. The thin linen of her dress clung to her exquisite curves, and her sash matched the shade of her plush lips.

A comfortable dress without frills, that one would wear at home. And so she was. In *their* home.

She caught him looking and blushed, but held his gaze. Good Lord, he had better snap out of it before he made a fool of himself. He turned his attention to the ceiling.

"It could do with some renovations but the beams"—he pointed upward—"they never lie. They can tell you whether a house is well-made. And these are sound and sturdy."

"Good, at least we won't have to worry about the ceiling collapsing on us," Stella said with a little smile. "And the decoration isn't *that* bad."

Jerome eyed the faded floral wallpaper and the cracked ochre tiles beneath their feet. "Kind of you to say so. Once Marbois's country house is completed and he gives me the rest of what is due, I should have enough to—"

She lay a hand on his arm. The gold band on her finger caught the fading light filtering through the window. "Please, Jerome. This is fine. You have already done so much."

She sidled closer to him. So close that he could wrap an arm around her waist and bring her mouth to his.

She is your wife now. Would that be so wrong?

He lifted his hand to touch her cheek. Her lips parted to take in a breath.

A loud wail came from the dining room. Stella turned, and Jerome let his hand drop.

"I should see if Clara and Jane find this place to their liking as well," she said.

He smiled. Besides the beams, another feature of the house had cemented his choice. "There's a small courtyard in the back. I wouldn't call it a garden, but at least Clara can play outside. Back when we lived in London, my sister Honorine suffered greatly from keeping the children indoors or having them play on the street."

Stella beamed at him, and warmth bubbled up in his chest. "Oh, how wonderful! That is most thoughtful of you."

The wailing grew louder. He watched as she walked away, hips swaying. Devil take it, how was he supposed to refrain from bedding her at the earliest opportunity?

No, she needed support. Delicate attention. She had only just said the words that made her Madame Stella Saint Yves. A period of adjustment was to be expected, and she could hardly adjust if he behaved like a starving beast.

Like so many men had before him. Including Ludlow.

He shook the thought away. Let that miscreant rot in London. Tonight, his wife would sleep soundly, safe in the house he had provided for her.

That is, if she wanted to sleep. After dinner, a stew of chicken and leeks with a creamy sauce, Jane retreated upstairs to the nursery with Clara, and he to the sitting room with the vague intention of catching up on his correspondence.

Stella followed him. He sat at the writing desk while she peered into the box he had left on the end table next to the divan.

"Are these all the books you own?" she asked, and from the corner of his eye, he saw her take one out and stroke the leather cover.

"Yes. Not nearly enough to fill the bookshelf. My father had an impressive library in Chartres when I was young, but we couldn't burden ourselves with books when we left."

And Honorine and Antonia had returned to find all of them stolen, along with anything that could be easily carried off and sold. They were lucky no one was squatting in the house, or worse. A few paintings of no great value had even remained on the walls, covered in dust and moldy on the edges, but relatively intact.

"I had books as well that I had to leave behind," Stella said, and picked up another volume. "Nothing so serious as *The Theory of Social Reform of the Marquess of Vauban*. I'm rather fond of poetry and novels."

"You would get along well with my sister Antonia. More often than not, she has her nose in a book. I will ask her for recommendations, if you like."

"I do enjoy reading before sleep. It helps ease my mind. Sadly, I haven't been able to indulge in that habit lately. Or indulge in anything, really."

Her voice, low and smooth, made the hairs on his neck stand on end. He rose from the desk to face her. Stella put the book down and tilted her head, her gaze dark and inviting.

"If you wish to retire, we must discuss our… sleeping arrangements," he said. "I have asked the maid to put your things in the room next to the nursery, and I took the street side room for myself. But if you prefer otherwise…"

Stella slowly walked over to him.

"You are always so considerate," she murmured. "That night at Imogen's party, when we left, you stopped me just as I was about to step into a puddle and took my hand to help me hop over it."

By God, how did she even remember this? He had no memory of it himself. At that point he had been half-crazed with lust, and it had taken every last bit of his self-control not to throw her down on the seat of the fiacre and have her before they had even arrived at her lodgings.

He certainly remembered *that*. And all the more because the need to control himself was tugging at his nerves at this very moment.

He swallowed, his cravat suddenly tight. "It seems only normal."

"To you, perhaps. I can assure you it is uncommon for most men to be as courteous towards someone they don't consider a lady."

Damn her, she was not helping. Because the images going through his mind were anything but courteous and considerate. She was so close now the scent of jasmine wafting off her heated skin filled his nostrils. With every breath she took her breasts strained at her bodice, the creamy skin quivering.

"I have always considered you as such," he replied, clinging to his own words for countenance. "Even if my actions may have said otherwise in the past. You are cultured and intelligent, and worthy of every regard."

Her rosy lips stretched into a smile. "Truly, Jerome, you are unlike any other man I've met."

She placed a hand on his chest, right above his heart. Could she feel it beating wildly under her fingers? She slid her palm up to his neck, and he leaned forward helplessly, his mouth hovering over hers. He was losing his footing. Losing his reason.

She is yours now. Take her.

He pressed his lips to hers. And drowned in the sensation. Her soft, plump mouth, moving in time with his, her fingers caressing his hair. God almighty, it was as if he'd been yearning for this kiss ever since the last one, months before. Longer, over a year. Too long. Too bloody long. His hands circled her waist to bring her flush against him. She groaned, her mouth opening, her tongue teasing his until their strokes grew more feverish.

By the devil, he was so hard that standing was almost painful. He tore his mouth away and buried his face in her neck to kiss and lick the sensitive skin. His fingers found her breast and squeezed. So soft, so perfect and heavy and sweet against his palm. He itched to tug at her neckline. To uncover those tempting rosy buds and suck them deep into his mouth.

Take her now. Do not bother with a bed. Anywhere will do.

"Jerome, *please*," Stella sighed. "If you wish to claim your rights as husband, wait no longer, I beg you."

He froze.

I have every right, boy. Every right to do as I damn well please with her, and if she has objections, she'll get another beating.

He closed his eyes. Pushed the memory back. But it was too late. Annette's tearful face, an angry snarl, blinding pain and then…

He straightened and grasped Stella's wrists, gently pushing her away. He had been about to lay his wife down on the divan of the parlor, spread her legs and take her there like some sort of brute.

Because it was his desire, and his right to do so.

A sickening sensation turned his stomach. He'd only just told her she was worth every regard, and yet he'd let his impulses overwhelm him once again.

"Forgive me," he said. "I did not mean to behave in such a manner."

Stella frowned, her beautiful face flushed. "What are you talking about?"

"I should not have forgotten myself as I did. It is not appropriate."

Maybe there was a more… respectable way to go about things. In a bed. Under the covers. In the dark. And he would treat her gently, reverently. Make her feel like a lady. Blast, how was he supposed to go about explaining all this?

"Stella, I think it would be wiser if…"

She shook her head. It was as if the light had gone out of her eyes.

"Please, leave it until morning. I am quite tired now."

He nodded. "Yes, of course."

"The room next to the nursery will be fine, thank you," she added, though her tone was dull and flat. "I bid you good night."

Well. That settled the question of sleeping arrangements. He should've felt relief. So why was he only left with bitter regret?

STELLA STRETCHED ON the fresh sheets and emerged from a deep slumber. She kept her eyes closed, her body still slack and heavy. Her first full night of uninterrupted sleep since leaving London. She inhaled and let out a slow breath. Oh, this was heavenly. Perhaps just another hour in bed… She had grown accustomed to rising late in the morning through the demands of her job. Surely Jerome would not begrudge her…

She groaned. *Jerome.* How was she supposed to face him?

In an instant, the sheets turned cold and brittle against her skin. She might have wakened next to him, wrapped in the warmth of his muscular arms, his solid chest against her back…

She would not only feel safe, but cherished. And all the better if her body was aching from a night of delicious lovemaking.

She ached now, though it was anything but enjoyable. Last night, anger and dejection had numbed her desire, and she'd let exhaustion drag her down into sweet oblivion as soon as her head hit the pillow. After a night of rest, however, the yearning throbbed once more between her legs, begging for relief.

Porca miseria, this could not stand. Attend to herself when she was newly married? Intolerable. She should find Jerome immediately and demand that he fulfill his husbandly duties. Surely it was unlawful not to honor his wife and deny them both such thrilling pleasure.

It would be just as devastatingly good this time. No, *better,* for longing heightened her senses, made every single one of her nerves tingle. She closed her eyes again. Her body hummed with need. She must do something, *anything,* to alleviate the burden.

She let her hand slide down her stomach to cup her mound over her nightrail. Her fingers moved quickly, pressed on her swollen bud, the friction from the fine linen igniting hot sparks in her belly.

If it were his hand… His fingers… Rough and deft at the same time. He would take his time to caress her, feeling his way between her slick folds, then slide a finger into her. Two. Moving deep, fast, while he leaned his muscular frame over her, his eyes locking with hers.

You are beautiful. So beautiful in your pleasure. Tell me what you desire.

She increased the pressure and let her legs fall apart, moisture saturating the thin cloth. He would fill her so perfectly. She'd felt his hardened length last night, thick and solid against her belly. If he had lifted her skirts, found her weeping for him… Circled her waist and set her on the divan… Turned her around so she could hold on to the backrest and *oh…*

Let me take you now. I cannot wait another moment.

His strong hands, gripping her waist, while he thrust inside her again and again, both of them panting. Grabbing a handful of her hair to make her head fall back, pulling, plunging deeper still, again, *again*, until…

Come for me, Stella.

Pleasure unfurled from her center, washing over her in waves while her muscles contracted. She chased the sensation until it receded, then rolled to her side.

Bliss gave way to turmoil. *Dio santo,* why could she not stop this incessant craving for him? Jerome had rejected her. He had married her, vowed to protect her, yet he could not bring himself to act on his desire as he had before. Why?

Ludlow. There could be no other reason for it. Jerome must be disgusted with the idea of bedding a woman who had also been bedded by a depraved blackguard. He'd spoken of Ludlow's reputation. Anyone working for him would have heard rumors, at least.

And the reality of it was far worse.

She tossed the covers back. Damn Ludlow. And damn Jerome as well, if he judged her for what she'd done in the past. Even if she admitted she had never let Ludlow near her, there had been other men. Men who had known his wife before he did. What gentleman would not be repelled at the thought?

Even if that gentleman had demonstrated to her that his desires were far from proper on the night they'd met, and had not been so polite when he was sinking into her from behind, grabbing her buttocks.

Be that as it may, she would not throw herself at his feet or bat her eyelashes at him over dinner. She would simply continue with their agreed-upon arrangement.

Once she was washed and dressed, she found Jerome at the dining room table. The object of her fantasy, calmly buttering a piece of bread, his long fingers moving back and forth with precision. Clearly, despite her best efforts she was not yet satiated, for they called all manner of forbidden images to mind. Such as what she'd just been doing not an hour previous. Goodness, she had better not watch his hands for too long.

"Ah, there you are," he said. "I was waiting for you to come down before going to work."

She took a seat in front of him. "I hope I didn't make you late."

"It is still quite early, though Clara and Jane have been up for an hour or so. They're playing in the courtyard. Did you sleep well?"

"I did. And you?"

He shrugged and bit into his bread, his tongue swiping his lower lip for crumbs. She watched him for a moment, and heat crept up her neck. *Enough of that.* She helped herself to a piece of bread and strawberry jam.

"So, it turns out Virginie Poulain is well enough to reprise her role as the Countess for the two remaining weeks of *Figaro*. Marcelline will be furious, of course. She may not be fond of me, but she detests Virginie."

She smiled, surprised at the warm, pleasant feeling it gave to discuss her doings with someone over breakfast. Not just someone—her *husband*.

"However, rehearsals are about to start for *Euphrosine*, and the director of the troupe told me I would be perfect for the part of Léonore."

Jerome set down his bread. "I thought you told me you would no longer work at the Olympique."

She frowned. "I told you I would no longer sing in *Figaro* after I collected my wages. I am lucky to be given a new opportunity."

He tapped his forefinger on the table. "You cannot possibly accept this offer."

His words stung like a slap. "Why not?"

"Why not?" He shook his head. "I can't escort you to the opera and back every night, and going alone would be too dangerous."

She dropped her spoon and glared at him, anger clawing its way up her throat. "I will be alone here all day while you are at work. How is that less dangerous?"

"You will be with Jane and the maid."

"And Clara, yes," she shot back. "If a nefarious villain breaks into the house, he will be scared witless and turn back immediately."

His brow furrowed. "Being in your own home in broad daylight, with neighbors about, is not nearly as risky as going alone to the Olympique and back in the middle of the night. Not to mention what goes on backstage."

She crossed her arms in front of her chest. "Is that why you don't want me to go? You fear I will let a man into my dressing room and fall back into my old habits?"

Jerome's eyes flashed, and his hand curled into a fist. Her words had hit their mark, but heaven help her, she was out of patience.

"No," he grated. "What I fear is you disappearing without a trace. I have gone to great lengths to put you out of harm's way, and I would appreciate if you did the same."

His reasoning was logical. But how could he not see that singing was more than just a way to earn a living for her? Singing was feeling. Living. Expressing all the emotions that swirled inside of her. Where did *his* emotions hide? How could he live like this, examining everything with cool calculation?

He wanted to keep her safe, yes. Yet the alternative he was offering was… nothing. "What do you expect me to do all day if I cannot perform?"

Jerome blinked at her, as if the question made no sense. "Read. Play with Clara. Discuss the menus with the maid. Even with hired help, my sisters always found things to do around the house."

"You told me Honorine has six children. I imagine she is quite busy indeed."

"Antonia enjoys needlework. Embroidery. She says it helps clear her mind. That is an occupation you could take up."

Words failed her. He was suggesting she replace her only

vocation, her only talent, the very thing that gave her a sense of worth, with needlework. Needlework! What could be worse than spending hours in a chair, stabbing at a piece of canvas until her eyes burned and her neck ached?

She glanced down at her plate. The urge to shatter the pretty piece of rose-patterned china crashing against the wall erupted inside her, but she clamped it down. No sense in breaking tableware that didn't even belong to him.

Jerome took out his pocket watch in apparent oblivion. "We can discuss this later. But surely you can see that singing at the Olympique is no longer feasible. You will have to write them a letter of resignation."

Tears filled her eyes, and she stared numbly at her food, fighting to contain the tempest of emotion within.

Jerome walked over to her and took her hand, giving it a small squeeze. "I know it is difficult. But I will provide for us now. It's better this way."

She snatched her hand away. *"Va' all'inferno!"*

He could certainly figure out on his own what that meant.

Chapter Ten

A FRACAS OF hammers and saws resonated in the summer air, pounding in time with the painful pulse in Jerome's forehead. He lifted the brim of his hat and swiped his handkerchief across his sweaty brow. By God, this heat was unbearable. If not for that and his blasted headache, he would have gladly joined in the work. He had before, on several occasions, and it never failed to clear his mind.

Marbois watched a group of masons tie a rope around a thick beam before lifting it up with the help of a pulley. "I'd say it's going rather well, wouldn't you?"

Jerome nodded. "We spoke with the head mason. They're making timely progress on the main frame. It won't be long until the brickwork can begin."

Marbois sighed in satisfaction and gazed at the grounds that were little more than a grassy stretch of land. They had arranged to spend the day in Belleville, inspecting the land, overseeing the masons' work and discussing the next steps of Marbois's colossal project.

"To think," he said, "this will soon be a domain that will make the Chateau de Malmaison pale in comparison."

Jerome laughed dryly. "Let's not get ahead of ourselves. But yes, I'm confident you will be most pleased with the result. After lunch, we can go over the latest plans."

Marbois slapped his shoulder as they started down the path towards the village. "Lunch, yes. I'm famished and parched. And no talk of work while we eat. You can tell me if married life has been treating you well. How is your lovely little opera singer?"

Annoyance flared within him at Marbois's choice of words, but to his credit, he had treated Jerome's situation with Stella, the baby and their precipitous marriage as nothing more than an amusing story, such as one might tell to entertain guests at dinner. Though Jerome hadn't disclosed the more alarming details to him, Marbois's open mind was all the more welcome that he had been very generous in his advance.

A few years ago, Jerome could only dream of such a sum. Now all he wanted to do was provide a comfortable life for Stella. One where she wouldn't have to toil daily like his sisters had during their exile, where she didn't depend on the whims of whoever employed her to survive. But evidently, he and his wife didn't see things eye to eye.

"Madame Saint Yves is well," Jerome replied shortly.

Marbois raised an eyebrow. "Come now, surely you must still be enjoying that newly wedded bliss."

"How would you know? You've never been married."

"I suspect it's quite like when one starts up with a new mistress and can hardly stay out of bed in her presence."

In this case, Marbois could not have been more wrong. For his bed had remained despairingly empty and cold since they had married three weeks past.

The ache in his forehead increased. The problem wasn't trying to figure out how to resume their intimate relationship in a delicate manner. No, the problem was getting his wife to speak to him. Touch him. Look upon him with warmth instead of muted anger, or worse, indifference.

He'd achieved his goal. Stella was safe at home with the baby. He clenched his jaw and kept his eyes fixed on the dusty path. Safe, yes, and unhappy.

What else could he possibly do? He hadn't heard anything new from Lefevre, but Ludlow and those in his employ were surely biding their time. The risk was too great. She could not return to the opera.

Over and over again, he repeated the words to himself, but sound logic frittered away when he watched Stella picking at her food despondently across the table, or cursing in Italian under her breath when he asked about her day. Like a wild bird trapped in a cage.

And he had been the one to trap her.

"I must say, you're not making a very convincing argument for monogamy," Marbois noted, breaking the silence. "Though you'll be surprised to hear that I've been courting the same woman for a few weeks now."

Jerome grunted. "Best of luck to you."

"Geneviève. A dancer at the Olympique, as it happens. Perhaps it would please your wife to meet with someone from the troupe."

Good Lord, the heat must be getting to Marbois as well. "Why the devil would it please her?"

The last thing Stella needed was a reminder of what she had left behind, though socializing with other people than Jane and the maid might lift her spirits.

"Listen, Paris is little more than a sweltering cesspool in July. Everyone who can afford to do so is fleeing to the countryside, at least for a few days. Do you remember Jacques Tremblay? The chap we met at *Figaro*?"

He wasn't likely to forget any detail of that night. Including Marbois's haughty business associate. "What about him?"

"He's having a get-together at his domain in Montmorency in a week's time. A house party. You know, fun and games." He elbowed Jerome's ribs. "And he's extremely fond of opera."

Jerome snorted. "The way you two kept prattling during the performance, I could never tell."

"I'm certain he would be overjoyed if your wife performed

for his guests. The two of you could come spend a few days and enjoy the fresh air. I will be there with Geneviève. And you could meet some potential clients."

Jerome glanced sideways at Marbois. His expression was the same as ever, a clever gaze and a half-amused smile. Still, best make sure there wasn't a catch.

"You're not trying to lure us into some sort of den of iniquity, are you?"

Marbois laughed. "My dear man, if there is one thing I pride myself in, it's never tricking anyone into *libertinage*. Believe it or not, most people come around to it themselves. I cannot guarantee it will all be proper behavior, but there are enough rooms in the house to accommodate those who simply wish to sleep."

Would there be enough for a newlywed couple to sleep apart? Stella would never agree to leave Jane and the baby alone in Paris, but even if she did, she would insist on separate rooms. Possibly ignore him outright. Who could blame her? Their marriage was in name only, and his presence brought her nothing but misery.

Blast, he needed to find something, *anything*, to alleviate her anguish, if only for a little while. He had bought her a stack of novels, yet they lay on the end table in the sitting room un-touched. He had ordered two new dresses and undergarments for her, as well as clothes for the babe. Stella had been charming to the modiste when she'd come to take measurements, and stiffly polite to him. At his wit's end, he had inquired into purchasing a pianoforte, but even second-hand, the instrument was far beyond his means.

Marbois's offer, on the other hand… A change of scenery would distract her at least. But then what to do about Clara? This wretched heat had also taken a toll on the little one, who wailed plaintively whenever she wasn't in Jane's arms, or her mother's. And if her swollen, reddened cheeks were anything to go by, the poor child was probably teething as well.

The questions tumbled around his mind fruitlessly. He would have to wait until he was done with Marbois to think properly, if his headache didn't grow any worse.

When he finally arrived back in Castellane Street, the sun was nearly set and the pain now held the entire right side of his head in a vice. Straight to bed, then. Chewing his supper would only bring a fresh wave of agony.

As he climbed up the stairs, a melodious voice, soft and smooth as velvet, drifted to his ears.

Brilla brilla la stellina, su nel cielo piccolina. Brilla brilla sopra noi…

Stella. His heart constricted. He slowed his pace and took care not to make the steps creak. He would not wish to interrupt her for the world.

Her bedroom door was ajar. She was sitting at the edge of the bed, facing away from him, cradling Clara in her arms and singing to her. The babe whimpered softly. Stella lowered her voice to a gentle murmur. The last light of the day filled the room with tender hues of orange and pink.

Jerome closed his eyes for a few moments. By God, her voice was just as heavenly when she sang a lullaby to her child as when she was on stage, performing a glorious aria in front of a crowd.

But now she had no choice. She had no one but Clara for an audience.

Guilt tore through him. She might have stolen a precious heirloom from Ludlow, but he was a thief of a different sort. He'd robbed her of what she loved most.

He opened his eyes again. And found Stella standing at the door, glaring at him, Clara still in her arms.

STELLA COULDN'T MOVE.

Jerome. Finally, he'd returned from Belleville after leaving at dawn. A twinge of relief pinched her heart, but she flicked it away immediately.

She should ignore him. March straight to the nursery to put Clara to bed, then back to her room, shutting the door behind her.

She had barely said a word to him in three weeks. True, he'd made halfhearted attempts to talk about trivial things, tried to please her with books, but he hadn't apologized. Nor had he recognized that he shouldn't have made the decision for her to stop singing. Nothing had changed, really.

Nothing, expect the way Jerome was looking at her now. His face was drawn, his eyes brimming with sorrow. He held on to the banister of the stairs, as if he was having trouble holding himself up. *Dio santo*, was he ill?

Her chest squeezed painfully. Her anger had been her anchor, strong and steady in the midst of her upturned life, but it faltered now. Jerome was distressed as well, and the desire to soothe him lurked at the edges of her mind.

Clara squirmed in her arms, her pudgy face squashed against Stella's bosom. Stella brought her finger to her lips, and Jerome nodded shortly. Then she tiptoed into the nursery. Clara hadn't settled after feeding, and Stella had taken her so that Jane could rest. She kissed the babe's downy forehead and gently placed her in her crib next to where Jane lay snoring softly.

When she came out of the nursery, Jerome had gone.

His room was empty. Blast. She could either go to bed and continue to give him the cold shoulder, or find him and hear if he had anything more to say for himself. He wouldn't seek her out. He was leaving it up to her. Giving her the choice.

She headed for the stairs.

He was in the sitting room, on the divan, leaning forward with his head in his hands. She walked over to him but stopped before she was close enough to touch him. The curve of his muscular shoulder and the fine linen of his shirt beckoned for her palm.

"Are you not well?"

"Bad headache," he muttered. "It's been a long, tiring day."

She clasped her hands behind her back. "Was your trip successful at least?"

He sat up and looked at her, frowning slightly. "The work on Marbois's house is on schedule, if that is what you're inquiring."

"Oh. That's good."

"Indeed."

Heavens, it had been much easier to converse with him when they were two strangers meeting at a party. If he had nothing else to say to her, she might as well go back upstairs.

"Marbois mentioned…"

Jerome closed his eyes briefly, as if bracing himself. Against the pain, or her reaction? Stella sat down in the armchair opposite the divan.

"He mentioned that one of his associates, Jacques Tremblay, was having a house party in Montmorency next week, and suggested we attend. Marbois will be there with his mistress. Geneviève, from the Olympique. Perhaps you know her."

Stella scoured her memory and dredged up the image of a blonde girl with large brown eyes. "Vaguely. But we cannot accept this offer in any case. First of all, I don't trust Marbois, nor do I wish to spend any more time with him than I already have."

"He's ruthless and he has little concern for proper behavior, I'll grant you. But if he wanted us to come to harm, he would have started by denying me an advance."

"Secondly," she continued, "I cannot leave Clara and Jane behind."

Thirdly, they would be going as a married couple and heaven help her, she did not have the willpower to share a bed with him and go quietly to sleep, pretending she didn't want him to pin her to the mattress.

Her anger may have overpowered her longing for a time, but that didn't mean it wasn't still simmering underneath. And it roused now as she watched Jerome. The light of the lamp sharpened his features, kindled the russet tones of his hair and trimmed beard. Her fingers yearned to reach out and cup his jaw.

Best to keep that quiet for now.

He nodded slowly. "I know. But Marbois thinks Tremblay will want you to perform for his guests. You could sing again. That is the only reason I did not refuse Marbois's offer outright."

Sing again. A fresh wave of anguish washed over her. A few songs at a house party wouldn't replace the opera. But had she not known it might come to this when she'd fled London? There had been no guarantee that she'd ever be able to perform again, and still she had gone through with it, because Clara was worth the risk.

Jerome might not understand how steep of a sacrifice it was. Yet he was trying to help the best he could.

Assembled guests, a pianoforte to accompany her. It wouldn't be much, but it would still be singing for people other than a baby. And God knew she was just about ready to burst with the need to make her voice ring out again.

She bit down on her lower lip. "That doesn't solve the problem of what to do about Clara."

"I've thought it over, and a trip to the countryside would also do her good. And Jane as well. They could travel to Chartres and stay with my sister and her family for a few weeks."

Clara, stay with Honorine? What made him think his sister would accept? He hadn't told her anything about his family's reaction to their marriage.

"The road from Paris to Chartres is safe, and the house has more than enough rooms to accommodate them. Clara could play in the garden, and her cousins would be only too happy to help take care of her."

The vision of Clara crawling on lush grass, surrounded by flowers and a gaggle of rosy-cheeked children, was almost too perfect to contemplate. But then another vision replaced it. Jane and Clara cowering in a carriage while a stranger threatened them. A pair of hands grabbing her and running through the night. Stella shook it away, her heart thumping.

"They cannot possibly travel there alone," she said. "It's far too dangerous."

As she said the words, they echoed Jerome's own words to her. *Too dangerous.* Were those the sort of dreadful images he saw in his mind when he imagined her going to the opera?

"We could arrange for an escort. But there's no need to decide now. Let us sleep on it." He forced his mouth into a faint smile. "If you'll excuse me, I really must go lie down."

"Yes, of course. I hope you feel better tomorrow."

Jerome rose from the divan. Her gaze remained on him as he left. No need to follow too closely after him, for sleep would certainly elude her tonight.

Chapter Eleven

"MESSAGE FOR YOU, *monsieur*."
A skinny boy slipped a small envelope into Jerome's hand, just as he was about to enter his shop. Jerome opened it in his study.

Urgent business. Come right away. Prevost's barber shop, north gallery of the Palais Royal. – NL

Damn and blast. He must get on with his work, especially if he was to make the trip to Montmorency with Stella next week. True, she hadn't agreed to it yet. She'd only just come down when he was about to leave for work, leaving no time for anything other than a polite goodbye, but by God, he would manage to convince her.

They needed a few days of respite. And he needed to make his wife trust his good intentions. If they could only live together in complicity and harmony in their daily life, their marriage would be better than many, and it would be enough for the time being.

But now this. Lefevre wouldn't summon him for mere a trifle. He crumpled the piece of paper and glanced at his pocket watch. It was early still, and his associates hadn't yet arrived. The sooner he left, the sooner he'd get back and start on his work.

Strange, though, that Lefevre had asked him to come to a barber shop instead of Saint Aphrodise.

By the time he reached the arcades of the Palais Royal, his face was burning and sweat was trickling down his back. It wasn't a long walk by any means, but in this blasted heat, with carts and vendors clogging the streets, it felt twice as arduous. Now where the devil was Prevost's barber shop?

He meandered in the maze of narrow alleyways for several minutes before finding it. The storefront only bore the name *Prevost—Barbier* in gray paint, and the glass pane was grimy, with nothing to attract the eye of potential clients. He knocked on the door and peered inside. The shop was deserted.

A few moments later, a man with dark longish hair and a dark scowl opened. Jerome straightened his shoulders. Blast, he was a big fellow, almost as tall as him and burlier. A thin scar ran across his left cheek, and his knobby nose looked like it had been broken in the past. Perhaps more than once.

"Jerome Saint Yves. I'm here to see Lefevre."

"Come in."

The man stepped aside, and Jerome entered the shop. Surprisingly, it did smell of soap, and a table and chair were set up in front of a large mirror. The man may look like he had just escaped from Bicêtre prison, but he was indeed a barber.

He led Jerome to the back of the shop through a small wooden door that opened onto a much larger room. A row of crates lined one wall, and in the center stood a round table. The only light came from a lamp at its center.

Lefevre sat with another man whose head drooped on his chest. Jerome squinted. Tied to a chair. This was his urgent business.

Lefevre stood and smiled cheerfully. "Good morning, Saint Yves. Glad you could come on such short notice. Have you two gentlemen been properly introduced?"

"Come off it, Nicolas," the barber growled.

"Raoul Prevost gives the best cut in the neighborhood," Lefevre continued with a sly grin. "Quick and clean, if you're ever in need of one."

"I'll keep it in mind," Jerome replied, then nodded towards the table. "Who's that?"

"Name's Camus. He hired the two thugs and sent them to Stella's door."

Fury bubbled up inside his chest but he fought to contain it. "Did he tell you anything?"

"Only that the Kingfisher gave him precise orders. The men were supposed to frighten your wife into leaving the city, but under no condition were they allowed to physically harm her. The Kingfisher wanted her… intact, for lack of a better term."

The sweat on Jerome's back turned to ice. *Intact.* Like a doll you didn't want to damage, in order to break her yourself. Or worse, have others break her for you, and pay for the right to do so. Yes, Ludlow would want her beautiful face untouched.

He struggled to push the words from his throat. "Anything else?"

Nicolas crossed his arms in front of his chest. Though he was still smiling, his gaze sharpened. "It took me awhile to get that out of him, not to mention that he didn't come quietly when I caught him. I thought you might want to ask him a few questions once he woke from his little nap."

Camus was half-snoring, half-mumbling, drool dribbling down his chin to land on a sweat-stained shirt. An angry red bruise marred his cheekbone. Jerome sat next to him. By God, what he wouldn't give to finish the job himself.

He grabbed a handful of hair, jerking Camus's head back. He yelped, and his eyes shot open. They rolled wildly in their sockets for a moment before landing on Jerome.

He tightened his grip. "You work for the Kingfisher."

Camus's face twisted into a grisly scowl. "Go fuck yourself. I already told you."

"It wasn't a question. Why was he after Stella Cardinelli?"

"That whore…"

His anger roared free. He bolted to his feet and kicked Camus's chair. It crashed to the ground. Blood pounded in his ears and his hands curled into fists, trembling to bash the man's face in.

Lefevre righted the chair. "Now, now, that's no way to stay alive. In fact, one more insult out of you and the last thing you'll hear is your skull cracking under this *monsieur's* boot."

Camus spat on the ground. "You think you can take down the Kingfisher. He's got men on his payroll from Cherbourg to Dunkirk."

Jerome seized the collar of the man's filthy shirt. "I don't give a bloody damn about your employer. I want to know how he got hired to chase after my wife."

Camus looked him up and down, as if weighing his options. His gaze flicked from Lefevre to Prevost, before halting on his own feet.

"The Kingfisher sometimes gets his hands on objects that turn a pretty profit in England," Camus muttered. "Little statues, old books, trinkets, things that belonged to *aristos* before they got their heads chopped off."

Jerome frowned. This sounded similar to Marbois's business, only as far as Jerome knew, Marbois specialized in furniture, jewelry and china, and his customers were French.

"He's got a contact in London who finds customers in return for casks of wine. He calls him the Marquess, but I don't know his real name."

No matter. Jerome could easily fill in the gap. Helping smuggle artifacts out of France and receiving contraband wine in return was only two more items to add on a long list of Ludlow's moral ills. The confirmation of his suspicions should have brought relief, except fury and disgust eclipsed every other emotion.

"And what is the Marquess planning on doing next?"

Camus shook his head. "You think the Kingfisher told me? I had my orders. Make the… lady leave Paris, so he could get her to the Marquess. That's it."

Nicolas gripped the backrest of Camus's chair. "Makes no sense. Why the hell didn't he just pay someone to take her?"

By the devil, the thought of some thug grabbing Stella threatened to set his blood to boiling. Twin urges warred within him. One pushed him to beat the man in front of him senseless, while the other pressed him to rush home and gather Stella into his arms. Feel her warm and solid and *there*, safely against him. Even if she ended up pushing him away and cursing at him, he'd revel in the sight of her.

An odd noise intruded on his thoughts. Laughter. Camus was *laughing*. A dry sound that was more like a bark, but his mouth stretched into a vicious grin.

"You know why, Lefevre. Paris is the Bone an's territory. Anyone can hire men to use their fists, but someone who can make a person disappear without a trace... You want that sort of skill, you have to go through the Bone Man first. He owns everyone in this fucking city."

The light left Lefevre's eyes. The lines on his face hardened. It was as if a mask had fallen and made every trace of his pleasant demeanor vanish.

He grabbed a switchblade from his pocket and flicked it open. Camus's face lost its color. Behind Jerome, Prevost drew in a sharp breath.

The blade flashed. A moment later, the ropes tying Camus fell to the ground.

"Not everyone," Lefevre said, his tone cold and deadly. "Get out of here before I gut you. And tell your master that anyone who gets too close to Stella Cardinelli will pay for it with his life. I'm only sparing yours so you can pass the message along."

Camus stood on shaky legs, and Prevost grabbed him by the collar and dragged him out of the room.

Lefevre closed his knife and drew several long breaths. Jerome waited in silence. He had no idea who the Bone Man was, but better wait for Lefevre to calm himself before asking.

"Well then," Lefevre finally said. "We now have a crucial bit of information. The Kingfisher will have to ask the Bone Man for help if he wants to get to Stella."

"You know this man?"

Lefevre's impish expression had returned. He sighed. "Unfortunately, yes. We go a long way back, to put it succinctly. But this will help me keep tabs on him, as long as you stay in Paris."

"I was considering attending a house party in Montmorency with Stella at Jacques Tremblay's estate."

"Fifteen kilometers north. Shouldn't be a problem, but stay close to your wife, eh?"

He was counting on it. More than Lefevre could possibly know. "Jane and the babe, however, would have to travel to Chartres to stay with my sister. Stella fears for their safety."

Lefevre rubbed his chin. "I can ask one or two of my pupils to escort them, if you like. With pistols. You'd have to pay for their way, of course."

"Trustworthy fellows, I assume?"

"Fellows who usually owe me a favor, or two, or three, which I find is the best sort of trust." He smiled. "I promise they'll be on their very best behavior."

"One look from Jane should be enough to cow them, in any case."

He'd received his fair share of disapproving glares from the nurse these past three weeks. But God willing, that was all about change.

Chapter Twelve

A S SOON AS the carriage started to move, a fresh spate of tears rose to Stella's eyes. She watched through the window as the house on Castellane Street disappeared in the distance.

Earlier that morning, she'd put on a brave face in front of Jane when she'd left with Clara, accompanied by a young man who was both soft-spoken and a veritable giant, taller than Jerome by almost a head. Their escort to Chartres. At least they would have some degree of protection, but oh, it tore her heart from her chest to imagine she would not see Clara, hold her or hear her gentle babbling for a few weeks.

A few weeks. An eternity, really. But Honorine was happy to take in Jane and Clara, and she had insisted that they stay until the weather was cooler, for the good of the baby. Jerome had let Stella read the letter herself. Edifying, to say the least.

Everyone here is very eager to meet the newest addition to the Saint Yves family. As Antonia pointed out in her last letter, Clara will be quite close in age to one of the children. Fortunate indeed! Might we be so lucky as to meet your wife soon as well? You will not be surprised to hear, dear brother, that Antonia and I have agreed she must be quite a formidable woman if she managed to turn your head.

Her stomach clenched painfully at the idea of meeting Jerome's family. They were good, honest people. They were welcoming Clara into their home as one of theirs, regardless of the circumstances of her birth and Jerome's hasty marriage to an opera singer. *Clara Saint Yves.*

Stella stared down at her hands, her vision blurred. She was deceiving them. Out of necessity, but it was a lie nonetheless. And she was deceiving Jerome as well. She was not a formidable woman by any means, quite the contrary.

Jerome frowned. "What is the matter?"

Stella dabbed her eyes with her handkerchief. "I miss Clara, that is all."

"Of course. I am sorry it is causing you distress, but she and Jane will be in good hands at my sister's house."

A brief smile passed over his lips, and he continued to look out the window in silence. They could not sit very far apart in the hackney, but his body was rigid in his seat, his shoulders slightly hunched.

As if he dared not move closer or take her hand to console her. Well, this was her doing. How could she ask for comfort now after treating him so coldly? They were back on speaking terms, at least, but Jerome still behaved as if she were ready to shatter in a million pieces if he was too direct. Or got too near.

"I know it's for the best," she said. "I hope you thanked Honorine on both our behalves for her kindness."

"I did, though you will be able to thank her yourself when we retrieve Clara at the end of the summer. Or whenever we may travel safely to Chartres."

Porca miseria, if she made it to the gates of the city without losing her breakfast, it would be a miracle. Jerome had not gone into the details of his latest conversation with Nicolas Lefevre, but knowing that Ludlow was working in tandem with a dangerous smuggler to get to her was more than enough.

She pressed her palm to her forehead and closed her eyes. Jerome turned towards her.

"Are you ill? Do you wish to stop?"

"No, no, I…" She took a deep breath. "I just need to rest."

"I heard Clara crying several times during the night. She must have awakened you as well. Did you go to her?"

Stella nodded. Usually, Clara's cries barely broke her slumber, and the babe quickly went back to sleep after Jane nursed her. Last night, her nerves were in such disarray that she simply had to make sure Clara was well, to hold her and soothe her until she was asleep in her arms.

Jerome's hand inched closer to hers. He hesitated for a moment, then gently took it in his.

"I can only imagine how difficult it must be, parting from your daughter. Most women of higher birth do not hesitate for a moment to leave their baby with a nurse in the countryside, and barely see their child for months on end. But you…" He pressed her fingers. "It is a testament to what a loving mother you are."

Oh heavens, she could endure it no longer. She pulled her hand away and covered her mouth to stop another sob from spilling out.

Jerome raked his hands through his hair. "I beg of you, Stella, tell me what is wrong and tell me truly." He spoke quickly, almost breathlessly. "I cannot bear standing by helplessly while you drown in misery. By God, it is enough to drive a man to madness."

Stella shook her head. "There is nothing you can do. I have brought this situation upon myself from the moment I left London."

His hands fell back down to clutch his knees, and he leaned forward, his body trembling with furious energy. "We will deal with Ludlow and his cronies. I promise you. When we are done with them, they will not approach within a league of you."

She bit her lower lip. She had to tell him now. She did not have the strength to keep up this charade. "There's something else, Jerome. Something about Clara. *Dio santo*, I do not know how to tell you this."

He watched her intently. "You are my wife. Whatever it is, your secrets are safe with me, always."

Dear God, let him still feel the same after her confession. She crossed her arms in front of her and took a quivering breath.

"My mother moved us from Milan to Covent Garden when I was very young. She trained me to be a singer like her, and also taught me how to secure protectors. It's a skill you must learn if you want to do more than simply survive."

You can have everything, cara mia. Everything you desire. Jewels, gowns, even a townhouse. These men only want two things in return: your beauty and your submission.

Mamma would know. She had been beautiful enough in her day to amass a small fortune, though her lavish tastes had left her with nearly nothing in the end. And she had been counting on Stella to support her.

"When you and I met, I had been without a protector for a few months. Shortly after Imogen's party, Ludlow started showing an interest in me. He sent me flowers, jewelry, extravagant gifts. Mamma was pressing me to accept him, but something in that man's eyes…"

The memory alone made her skin crawl. His deadened gaze, his cruel smile, his fair hair glistening with pomade… She shuddered.

"I would not let him touch me. Not for the world. But everyone in the troupe assumed I would become his mistress, given his wealth. Then, one night after a performance, a young dancer came to my dressing room. Her name was Lilian. A wisp of a thing, barely fourteen, with vivid red hair. So pretty and graceful."

She could see the girl now, clear as day. The way she wrung her hands, her large blue eyes filled with fear.

"She wanted to warn me about Ludlow, she said. He'd invited her to come to his home, promised her a pretty necklace and a new dress. She thought she could not refuse a man so wealthy and powerful. You can imagine what that *débauché* did to her."

Jerome closed his eyes for a moment. "Damn him. Damn him to hell."

A vise gripped her throat. She swallowed and went on. "She was with child. As soon as it became apparent, she was dismissed. No one in the troupe batted an eye. No one helped her. Her family had spurned her, and she was left to fend for herself. Meanwhile Mamma kept badgering me to give myself to Ludlow."

The carriage lurched on. Stella rested her forehead against the window pane, her gaze following the rows of buildings as they passed.

"I set out to find Lilian. I couldn't stand the idea that she alone must bear the consequences of an evil man's crimes. She was living in a filthy tenement in Saint Giles and by then, she was close to her confinement. With what savings I had, I rented a cleaner room for her, bought her food. But it was all in vain. She died shortly after giving birth to a little girl. She named her Clara and made me promise to take care of her."

Tears rolled down her cheeks. She dared not look at Jerome. The clomping of the horses and rattling of the wheels resonated in the cab, but the silence between them lay thick and heavy.

"I could not simply leave Clara at a foundling hospital. She would have ended up in the workhouse, if disease hadn't taken her first. But I could not stay in London either. I needed to escape Mamma, to take Clara far away from Ludlow. Nowhere in England was safe. I hired Jane and prepared to leave for France. But I did not know how far we would have to go, and I needed money. So I finally agreed to meet Ludlow alone at his home. He served me wine, and I waited for the right moment to get my hands on what I could. He had bragged about that damned box worth a king's ransom more than once, so I asked to see it. He was already deep in his cups, thank God. Then, when he was off retrieving it, I drugged his wine so he would fall unconscious."

She ground her teeth. She should have killed that bastard then and there, or used a stronger poison. A single solid blow with a candlestick... But being wanted for murder would not have helped Clara in the slightest, no matter how much Ludlow deserved to die.

"I took the box and some banknotes and fled. I had left a few items with Jane and told her to be ready. Within the hour we were on our way to Calais."

Jerome knew the rest of the story. The tension in her chest eased, though dread rushed into the empty space. She dared a glance at him. He sat still, gaze fixed in front of him, as if deep in thought.

"Forgive me for not telling you sooner," she said. "I know I should have, but I was afraid you might change your mind."

He frowned. "You thought I wouldn't marry you if I knew?"

"I couldn't take that chance. I would do anything to keep Clara safe."

"Yes. Because you are her mother."

No words had ever touched deeper or shone brighter inside of her than what he had just said. "Jerome…"

His gaze caught hers, clear and strong and steady. "I am grateful you told me the truth, but it changes nothing. You are Clara's mother, Stella. In every way that matters. No one who has seen you with her could doubt it, not for a single moment. And neither should you."

How she wanted to slide over to him, press herself against him, and kiss him senseless. But lingering fear held her back. He had rejected her once when they'd kissed in the sitting room, and a carriage was hardly a more appropriate place for intimacy.

Jerome smiled. "You can rest now. Lean your head on my shoulder if you wish."

What she really wanted was his arms, wrapped around her, his solid warmth surrounding her. But she was too exhausted to ask. His shoulder would have to do until they arrived.

"JEROME SAINT YVES, pleasure. And this is my wife, Stella Saint

Yves."

Jerome had repeated the same words twenty or so times that afternoon as they were introduced to Tremblay's guests. And every time, possessiveness rushed from his belly to warm the rest of his body. Having Stella at his arm, fanning herself lightly as they exchanged pleasantries with strangers, her lips curled into a charming smile…

A real smile. She had slept all the way from Paris to Montmorency, neatly tucked against him, and had roused from her nap when the carriage stopped in front of Tremblay's sturdy neoclassical mansion. Her expression was rested. Almost serene. And the heavy-lidded look she'd given him had shot immediately to his groin. She'd woken up in his arms that fateful morning wearing the same expression.

How on earth had he found it in himself to leave?

Now he could barely stand to let her out of his sight. Emotions reeled inside his mind. Regret that she'd felt the need to hide Clara's parentage from him. Relief that she'd never been subjected to Ludlow's appetites. Fury at the destruction that whoreson had wrought on so many lives.

Stella was the only thing tethering him. Her soft laughter, her floral scent, the warmth of her hand on his arm, all of it made his thoughts melt away to leave room for his senses.

"Glad you could make it, Saint Yves," Tremblay told him as they stood on the stone terrace overlooking the gardens, hilly slopes planted with a palette of colorful bushes and trees, and a winding path leading to a large pond. "When Marbois suggested your wife might entertain us tonight, I knew I must send you an invitation."

"We thank you warmly, *monsieur*," Stella said. "I am looking forward to performing."

"Oh, there's Marbois now with Geneviève."

Marbois waved at Jerome. At his arm was a willowy blonde woman with large brown eyes. She greeted Stella excitedly, as if they were long-lost friends.

"It is so lovely to see you! I was very upset when you left and Virginie came back, of course it was her role to begin with, but I dare say I thought you were much better …"

She spoke very quickly, her hands fluttering about. Stella simply smiled politely.

"Oh, and do you know Marcelline is here too? With Girard, naturally. He bought her a new emerald bracelet. It's to die for, simply to die for!"

Marbois patted her hand. "Now, now, my sweet, don't get too excited."

Stella raised an eyebrow. "I did not know Marcelline was in attendance. I doubt she will be as pleased to see me."

"Nonsense! Perhaps the two of you could sing a duet? Oh, wouldn't that be wonderful!"

"Wonderful? If she agrees to share the stage with anyone, it would be nothing short of miraculous."

Marbois sighed and gently led Geneviève away. "Come along, my sweet, let us take a turn around the garden. The shade might help you cool down."

"Yes, even here, the heat is abominable," Stella said. "Perhaps we could return inside?"

Jerome followed her lead back to the marble hall. Her fingers wrapped more tightly around his arm. His head was spinning faintly. "Would you like to go up to the room and lie down?"

His voice was raspy. By God, what he wouldn't give to drag her up there and spend the rest of the day, evening and night in bed with her, Tremblay and his guests be damned. But she had come here to sing above all else.

She smiled at him, her cheeks a rosy hue. "I am quite rested, thank you, though I should probably practice a bit before tonight."

He nodded slowly. "Do you wish me to stay with you?"

Her smile softened. "I will be safe in our room, don't worry. And besides…" She hesitated and gave a breathy little laugh. "If you are with me, I fear it will affect my concentration."

His mouth went dry. His gaze darted to her mouth, her breasts, then back up to her eyes. One kiss, just one kiss, and his self-control would snap like a string wound too tightly.

"As you wish," he managed. "I will wait for you downstairs."

And a long and tedious wait it was. Listening to Marbois describe his latest sales and discussing architecture with a few of the guests as they mingled in the sitting room wasn't much of a distraction. His body hummed with nervous energy, urging him to go above stairs and see for himself how Stella was doing.

The sun was nearly set. Ladies started to filter into the room, wrapped in colorful satin and gauze, bejeweled and coiffed, reticules hanging from their arms. When Stella finally appeared, his heart froze in his chest. Then started again, pumping blood through his veins in a mad rhythm.

Her hair was a crown of silky curls, and she was wearing one of the new dresses he'd ordered for her, a dark green silk gown lined with gold braid. On paper, the design had looked stylish and befitting for a lady. On her, it was magnificent. Queenly. The silky fabric shimmered in the candlelight with every sway of her hips and the bodice gently pushed up her breasts over the dipping neckline. All she was missing was a sparkling bracelet at her wrist, a necklace of precious stones at her throat.

But all the jewels in the world could not have made her more stunning. And the expanse of bare skin enticed him, made his mouth tingle with the memory of its softness, made him want to trace his tongue from the top of her breasts to the curve of her ear.

Their gazes met. She took in a breath, lips parted. He did not look away.

If she saw the desire in his eyes, all the better, for he would not wait beyond tonight before claiming what was his.

Chapter Thirteen

N OT EVEN THE slightest cheat before the highlight. Marcelline sustained the entire phrase through a single breath, in perfect control, building the note until it echoed off the walls. Stella could only admire her impeccable technique. When the note finally faded, Marcelline brought her arms to her sides, and applause erupted. She smiled triumphantly and blew a kiss to Girard, who was seated right in front of Stella.

"Beautiful, my darling," the pot-bellied man exclaimed.

Stella clapped along with everyone else, but her insides fluttered. Marcelline had performed the most difficult aria from *Euphrosine*. Naturally, that *stronza* had insisted on singing first. She'd barely greeted Stella when they had finally met at dinner, her gaze filled with undisguised contempt. No doubt hoping it would put more pressure on Stella before her own performance. In this respect she had achieved her goal.

Beside her, Jerome leaned in, his lips nearly brushing her ear. "Do not fear. You will do splendidly."

A delicious shiver tickled the length of her neck. "What makes you think I am afraid?"

She felt him smile. "You've been tapping your fan on your thigh since we took our seats."

His hand found hers and gave it a little squeeze. The fluttering quickened, but this time it had nothing to do with nerves.

Marcelline sashayed to her seat next to Girard. "I believe it is your turn now, Bianca." She covered her mouth with the tips of her fingers. "Oh, pardon me, I meant Stella, of course. You have no further need of your stage name now."

Stella rose from her chair and smoothed down her dress. "Oh, but I so miss singing in *Figaro* that I picked an aria from the fourth act. One you must know quite well. *Deh vieni non tardar.*"

Marcelline's smile vanished. "But… That is Susanna's part! *My* part!"

"*Was* your part, my dear," Stella replied, sidestepping Jerome to advance to the front of the conservatory. "Now it belongs to any soprano who happens to know the lyrics."

Marcelline took her seat and crossed her arms in front of her. Her annoyance was gratifying, but in truth, that wasn't the reason Stella had chosen this aria. A lovely song, one she had sung many times, yet the lyrics had never struck her as they did now.

She took her position and met Jerome's gaze. It was fixed on her, unflinching. Smoldering with unspoken desire, just like the night they had met.

Though he did not speak Italian, she would sing every word for him. She straightened her shoulders, swept her gaze over the audience, and inhaled deeply.

Deh vieni, non tardar, o gioja bella
Vieni ove amore per goder t'appella…

She let the languid notes flow through her belly, her chest, pushing them forth from her very core. They spoke of unbridled passion under cover of the night, the irresistible temptation to let oneself be swept away.

Oh, come, don't be late, my beautiful joy
Come where love calls you to enjoyment…

Bliss swelled, rolled through her, rose as one with the melody, all the way up her throat, past her lips. She closed her eyes.

Ai piaceri d'amor qui tutto adesca…

When she opened them again, she once more caught Jerome's gaze.

Here, everything entices one to love's pleasures…

The raw hunger swirling in his gray eyes nearly caused a hitch in her breath. She forged ahead, her voice growing stronger, her pitch ascending, until it mellowed again on the last delicate notes of the aria.

Silence surrounded her for half a second. Her own heart pounded with wild joy in her ears. Then the applause erupted around her. Her audience numbered fewer than twenty, but the noise was as sweet as an entire opera house cheering. She bowed and smiled at them, left, right, even at Marcelline, whose lips were now puckered in a bitter grimace.

"Magnificent!" Tremblay called out. "*Madame*, I demand an encore."

"That is too kind of you," she said, and glanced at Jerome. His eyes had darkened, and his jaw was clenched, but not with anger. With impatience.

"I could accompany you on the pianoforte this time," Geneviève suggested. "Oh, do say yes! Something by Rameau, perhaps?"

How could she refuse? After all, she had been invited here to sing. But heaven help her, the elation of her performance begged to be channeled elsewhere. Into the bedroom, and without delay.

She kept her smile in place. "Of course."

One more song, then Girard suggested that Marcelline should have another turn. Stella returned to her seat, and Jerome grabbed her hand, his grip tight around her fingers.

"We shall retire as soon as she finishes."

Dio santo, the fluttering had now taken over her entire body.

"I very much doubt Marcelline will stop there."

"I don't give a damn if she wants to sing an entire opera," he growled under his breath. "One song, that's it. Do you understand me?"

There it was. The harsh, commanding tone she'd teased out of him with every stroke, every touch, every kiss, the first time she'd taken him to bed. And it had the same effect on her now, melting her insides and rousing the throbbing ache between her legs.

Yes, no more than one song. Each successive note already prolonged this delectable torture, until her desire was fighting furiously within, demanding to be set free. Any more, and she'd have to give it free rein.

Mercifully, after Marcelline's performance, Tremblay called for wine and cognac. The guests rose from their seats, and Jerome placed his hand on the small of Stella's back to guide her towards the door.

One of the gentlemen, skinny and gray-haired, stepped in front of them. "I was most impressed with your performance, *madame*. You sing exquisitely."

"Thank you, Monsieur..."

"Pierre Blondel," Jerome supplied in a clipped tone. "Monsieur Blondel and I discussed the three orders of Ancient architecture while I was waiting for you to come down."

The gentleman nodded. "Indeed, and a most enlightening conversation it was. One is always pleasantly surprised to make interesting acquaintances at parties. If you would care to join me..."

Jerome's fingers grazed her back and she breathed in sharply. "Later, perhaps. My wife is quite tired."

Blondel blinked and smiled politely. "Yes, of course."

Thank goodness, there was no one else to stop them as they exited the conservatory. They said nothing as they made their way up the staircase. Her desire weighed on her belly, her limbs, yet the urge to reach the bedroom overpowered it, and she quickened her steps. Jerome's hand never left her waist, and she leaned into him until their sides touched.

Near, so near. Not near enough. Three more steps, two, one...

They finally entered the cool, gray shadows of the bedroom. Moonlight shone softly through the window. Stella turned to Jerome, and he wrapped his arms around her, bringing her close. She lifted her hand to cup his jaw, her thumb grazing over his cheekbones, eyes searching his. His breath was short, but now that they were finally alone, a hint of doubt lingered in his gaze.

"Tell me what is wrong." She pushed onto her toes to kiss him. "Tell me, and let there be nothing left to hinder us."

"Stella..."

He leaned forward and caught her mouth. Slowly, almost gently, his body trembling, his hands slackening their grip.

"You are breathtaking," he murmured against her lips. "God help me, hearing you sing... I would have taken you in my arms right there and carried you to the room."

She smiled. "I would not have complained."

"But after all you've been through..." He shook his head. "You deserve to be treated with consideration. With delicacy."

She stroked the nape of his neck, the trimmed hair prickly under her fingertips. "You are afraid of hurting me?"

She read the answer in his eyes, and it stripped away the last of the defenses she kept around her heart. So that was why he'd held back. Ludlow or high-handed disgust over her past had nothing to do with it. He simply wished to be courteous towards his wife, to spare her any further discomfort.

The notion only fanned the pulsing longing that had taken her over. She kissed him again, grasping his wrist to bring his palm to her breast. He groaned, and his fingers flexed. Her nipple hardened to a peak, desperate for more friction.

"Tell me, husband," she purred. "Did you hurt me, the night I took you to bed?"

He swallowed thickly. "No."

"Did I not ask you to share your innermost desire with me?"

"You did."

She dipped her mouth to trail kisses on his neck. "And do you remember how I screamed with pleasure when you took me again and again? How I begged you never to stop?"

"By the devil, Stella."

She studied him. Something had shifted in his gaze. The doubt had vanished. All that was left now was fire, burning freely.

His other hand cupped her backside to press her closer. Right against his rigid staff. She whimpered as her hips jerked forward to rub the hard ridge against her center.

"Hardly a night goes by where I don't hear your cries in my mind," he rasped. "It has haunted me. Tormented me until I thought I was going mad."

"Then do not be gentle or delicate, Jerome. Take all that you want." She nipped his bottom lip teasingly. "Command your wife. And give her the same pleasure."

Their mouths met in a frenzied dance. Jerome's frantic fingers worked to divest her of her dress, to unpin her hair, to unlace her corset, coming just short of tearing them off in haste. When only her chemise stood between his gaze and her naked form, he broke away and stepped back.

"Take it off," he ordered in a low, growling voice that sent a fresh throb of yearning deep in her belly.

She lifted the fine material over her head. His gaze slowly traveled up her legs, paused at the triangle of dark curls, then up her stomach, her breasts, taking its time before finally meeting hers again. Heavens, he did not even need to touch to make slick moisture gather between her legs.

"Go lie on the bed."

She obeyed, dizzy with need. He stood at the edge of the bed, towering over her, eyes fixed on her body even as he undid the buttons of his waistcoat and pulled his shirttails from his breeches.

Stone. He was an architect, but it was as if his entire being was made of stone. Every last inch of bared skin proved as much. Smooth as marble, fully formed, whoever had sculpted his body was every bit the artistic genius as the great composers.

He did this. He sculpted himself.

She stared at him and knew it to be true. She'd felt the roughness and strength of his hands. And that strength, honed through hard work, translated to the rest of him. To his entire being.

The mattress dipped under his weight, as he stretched beside her. "Spread your legs and put your hands over your head."

Yes, anything. She would do anything he asked. With a single hand, he gripped both her wrists like a vise and pinned them into the pillow. Her heart thudded madly. Heavens, she thought she could not want him more, but he was pushing her to the brink.

His free hand stroked her face. "Tell me, did you think of that night as often as I did?"

"God, yes. I could not get it out of my mind."

"And were you aroused when you reminisced?"

She nodded and resisted the impulse to squeeze her legs together to relieve the searing ache. Oh, let him tend to it quickly, she could endure no more. "Always."

"How so? Describe it to me."

His hand traveled down her neck to her breasts. He rolled the sensitive tip between his thumb and forefinger, and she arched against his touch.

"I… I ached for you," she stammered, struggling for words. "So much… It caused me pain. I felt so empty, slick and ready for you and—*oh*."

His hand left her breast, slipped past her waist, and he thrust two fingers into her wetness. Her body surrendered to his so easily, and he sank in deep and deeper. Sparks of heat burst like small fireworks, gathered in her center as he thrust his fingers, in and out, in and out. She moaned with each thrust, wrists struggling against his grip but his hand only tightened. In and out, in and out, faster now, his palm pressing on the swollen core of her arousal.

"Is this what you have been craving?" he grated. "My fingers inside of you? My cock?"

"Yes, *yes*, don't stop…"

Close, so close. She needed more. Harder. Deeper. He tore his hand away and positioned himself between her legs, still pinning her wrists above her head.

"I want to hold you," she panted. "Touch you."

He kissed her, his tongue flicking, caressing, savoring. The head of his shaft pressed maddeningly against her entrance. "Ask nicely then, wife."

"Please, let me touch you."

He released her wrists, and her palms pressed into his back, urging him on. Muscles rippled under her touch. He eased in slowly at first his gaze locked with hers, then sheathed himself fully.

She cried out, eyes squeezing shut against the exquisite sensation of him filling her so completely and perfectly. His weight, the taut muscles working under her touch, the sharp pounding surge of his hips… White-hot flames licked at her, consuming from the inside, obliterating every thought and every word, leaving only sounds of ecstasy. His groans, her cries, the slapping of his skin against hers.

He withdrew suddenly. For a moment, she simply looked at him, breathless and confused, but he flipped her over.

He ran his palm over her spine, almost tenderly. "I want to take you like this. Bury myself deep as I can."

"Yes, *please* yes," she mewled.

He lifted her buttocks and entered her roughly. Hitting a spot inside that made her scream with wild abandon. She teetered on the edge, reaching desperately for her peak, until his fingers tangled in her hair, pulling just enough to mix prickles of pain to the boundless pleasure. Shards of light exploded in her vision, and her muscles quivered as bliss surged through her in waves.

He thrust once, twice, then stilled, buried to the hilt, spilling his seed inside of her. Then slumped to the bed, his sweat-soaked body shaking.

"Stella," he breathed, and pulled her to him. "My Stella. My love."

Chapter Fourteen

STELLA STOOD AT the window in a lacy chiffon peignoir, black curls tumbling freely down her back, skin creamy and radiant in the midday sun. Jerome shook off the last remnants of sleep as he drank in the sight.

Three meters away, more or less. Too far. They'd fallen asleep as the sky paled, his arms about her, their legs entwined, her chest rising and falling against his with every breath, his hands stroking her silky hair.

This time, he had no reason to depart at dawn—no lengthy trip ahead of him, no goodbyes. Ten years in London had been nothing compared to leaving her after one night. His life in England hadn't tightened his throat and filled him with a strange, lingering sorrow. No, that was all Stella.

No more. Stella was his, Stella was there. She turned to him and smiled, her gaze serene and still laced with drowsiness.

He stretched his arms and propped himself up on one elbow. "Come back to bed."

"It must be past noon already, and I am famished. Are you not as well, *mio amato?*"

He did not know the precise meaning of the words, but reveled in her soft, sensuous tone. He had taken her several times during the night, as if their lovemaking only sharpened his hunger for her instead of satiating him. Now lust rushed through his veins once more and roused his manhood.

"Famished, yes. Last night whetted my appetite. Come here."

Her shoulders sagged, and she emitted a breathy little groan. But then arousal sparked in her eyes. He stretched out his hand for her to take and pulled her to him.

She pushed at his chest in a halfhearted manner. "We cannot spend all day in bed."

He tugged at the bow that tied her garment at the side. "I'm the one who is supposed to be overly concerned with propriety."

"Exactly. If I cannot count on you to be reasonable, where does that leave us?"

Her peignoir fell open. By God, her voluptuous curves took his breath away every time. The fullness of her bosom, her shapely, creamy thighs and plump buttocks… All for his hands, his mouth, his tongue. He cupped her breast, thumb grazing over the pebbled tip. Her lips fell open in a groan.

"If you have any further arguments, my love, I would be happy to hear them."

She shook her head, lids half closed. "No, no."

He retrieved his hand. He had never been one to tease, but he found it was easy to provoke Stella in jest. Easy and supremely enjoyable. "No?"

A sigh escaped her, though her lips lifted in a half-smile. "I meant no arguments, you infuriating man. Don't you dare stop what you're doing."

"Good. Now take that off."

She let her peignoir fall to the floor, and he tilted her forward to catch her nipple with his teeth. She moaned, arching into him as he licked and flicked the dusky bud, then turned his attention to the other, sucking in earnest.

"Please," she whimpered. "Please, Jerome, take me now. Feel how ready I am for you."

She grabbed his hand to place it between her legs, but he tugged it free. His fingers would not do this time. He yearned for more.

"Wait." He grasped her hips and lifted her so she straddled him on the mattress, then trailed kisses on her stomach. "I want to put my mouth on you."

Stella froze and pushed him back, frowning. "Your mouth? Have you done this before?"

He nodded. "I had a… relation of sorts with a woman in London. A widow who enjoyed my company, and a French immigrant as well. We met sporadically over a year or so. She instructed me in certain techniques."

And he was not proud of having given in. Even now, a hint of shame niggled at him. Something else he had hidden from his family, but five years into their exile, distractions were few, and it was better than going to the brothel.

Or worse, taking a maid's innocence like he once had.

None of that. That is all in the past. All that mattered now was Stella, and how to make her sigh and purr and cry with pleasure.

"Well, in that case, you are more learned than I am," she said with a little laugh. Good Lord, was she nervous? "No man has ever made me that sort of offer."

Possessiveness flared inside of him. A damn shame for those fools, but all the better for him. He lay back, her legs on both sides of his chest.

"You don't have to do anything. Just stay like this."

She nodded, biting her lip. He edged lower until her slick folds were within reach of his tongue. He swiped it over the length of her, and she whimpered, her entire body tensing above him. He did it again, slowly, delicately, giving her time to get used to the sensation, though it was a struggle not to feast on her sweet taste.

"Is that pleasurable for you?"

"Yes. *Oh,* keep going, I beg you."

Devil take it, he was the one who should be begging her. He was like a man dying of thirst who had just been given a pitcher of the freshest, purest water. His fingers clenched around the pliant flesh of her thighs, and he lifted his head to take her bud into his mouth, sucking lightly at first. Her moans grew louder, higher, and she rolled her hips forward. He sucked harder. Her moans turned to cries, resonating with every breath she exhaled.

She raked her fingers through her hair and stilled his movements. He leaned back and looked up at her. Her cheeks were flushed, her gaze clouded.

"I am close," she panted. "I need you inside of me, Jerome. Now."

He lay back on the mattress, eyes fixed on her as she aligned herself with his erection. He had dreamed of this. Fantasized about it, over and over again. And it paled in comparison to the real Stella, a cheaply made copy compared to a vibrant masterpiece.

She was a masterpiece. So stunning when she hovered near her peak, her pale skin bearing a rosy glow of arousal and her black curls in disarray, that he couldn't tear his gaze away. She took his staff in hand and guided it to her entrance, lowering herself in one sharp stroke.

A loud groan tore from his throat. Pleasure reverberated throughout his entire body only to rush back immediately to his cock. The ebb and flow followed her movements as she rode him, and he surged up to meet her, fast and hard, her lush breasts bouncing with each thrust.

"More, *please*, more," she cried.

He gave it to her. Everything, with all the vigor he could muster, until she clenched tightly around him. Too much, the sensation was too much. His muscles contracted until tension unfurled in his belly, sending hot waves of pleasure shooting forth.

They slowed their movements, both of them breathless. Stella slumped forward and curled up on his chest.

She fit so perfectly there, cradled in his arms. Limp with the pleasure he had given her, his manhood still inside her.

A sliver of hesitation worked its way through his contentment. He hadn't asked her if she wanted him to take precautions, and neither had she requested a gentleman's finish. They were married, after all. But they had not discussed the topic of children.

Children. A vivid vision burst to life in his mind. Stella holding a baby, and little Clara sitting next to her, a year or two older, eager to take her sibling's tiny hand in hers.

His family. *Their* family. Yes, it was right, so right that it felt like a distant but tangible reality on the horizon, calling to him.

"Are you still famished, my love?" he asked, gently pushing a strand of hair back behind her ear.

"For food, yes," she replied, and crept up to kiss him. "As for the rest, I might be sated for a little while, so let us get dressed while we still can."

⇥⟫⟪⟻

Stella inhaled deeply. The air was saturated with the sweet scent of carnations and hortensias.

"What lovely gardens. Are you considering something similar for Marbois's grounds?"

She and Jerome were strolling along a path that led to a pond. A rainbow of flowering bushes lined the path, and the leaves of hornbeams and ash rustled in the breeze, providing patches of shade.

"Marbois has indeed indicated he would like an English-style garden, like most people these days," Jerome replied. "But the landscaper will take care of it. I don't have much of an eye for gardens."

She leaned the side of her head on his shoulder. "Ah yes, you prefer stone. White facades, clean cut lines in perfect symmetry."

He paused and lifted her chin with his forefinger. "For houses, yes. But I have been known to favor vivid, untamed beauty elsewhere."

He kissed her, and she broke away with a smile. "I am glad to hear it. But if I were lucky enough to have such an estate myself, I would adore a garden such as this one. Everything calls to your senses—the scents, the vibrant colors, the sound of leaves. It sings to one's heart."

"Yes, just like the gardens in the fourth act of Figaro. *Here, everything entices one to love's pleasures.*"

She raised an eyebrow. "I thought you didn't understand Italian."

His mouth tilted in a teasing smile. "I don't. I just remember the lyrics from the French translation of the libretto."

She gently swatted his forearm with her fan. "You could have told me. I sang that aria for you, you know."

He caught her hand to press his lips on her knuckles. "I was hoping you did."

They continued along the path. Stella let the buoyant, heavenly sensation of being in Jerome's presence with nothing between them carry her. Any outside threats they would have to deal with once this idyllic stay was over still lurked in waiting, but together, facing them no longer felt like an impossible feat. And she was no longer lost, tossed about and uncertain where to land.

Her heart soared at the idea of another day, another night spent with him. And then many more days, many more nights. Safe in his arms, loving him freely.

Love. Such a curious, astonishing feeling, unlike anything she had imagined. She had sung of love onstage more times than she could count, she had playacted passion both in her performances and for her protectors. But it was nothing like this feeling of easy trust, of soft joy radiating through her with every look, every touch.

She tightened her fingers about his arm, the hard muscles rippling under her touch. The path curved to the left and revealed Marbois, Geneviève and Blondel walking the other way.

"Good afternoon," Marbois called. "Enjoying the view? I hope you're taking notes, Saint Yves."

"*Monsieur, madame.*" Blondel nodded. "What a fortunate

coincidence. I am sorry we could not speak longer yesterday. Perhaps now, if you have a moment."

My, this man was persistent, but so impeccably courteous it was hard to say no. "By all means, *monsieur*, we would be delighted."

"From what I have heard, you are currently not a part of any troupe?"

"Yes, and a shame too," Geneviève said. "Everyone adored her at the Olympique."

Untrue, but generous. Stella thanked her with a smile, while Blondel carried on.

"Well, as it happens, my very dear friend has just been named director of the Opéra Comique. I am certain I could arrange for you to meet him."

Stella blinked in surprise. "Oh. That is… most considerate of you, *monsieur*."

She glanced at Jerome. His mouth was a thin line and his eyes fixed a point over Blondel's shoulder, but he remained silent.

"I am not certain I am at leisure to perform in the coming weeks…"

"Really?" Blondel shook his head. "A shame. A voice like yours should not stay off the stage for such a lengthy period of time."

Jerome cleared his throat. "Yes. It is a shame. And I will work to resolve this issue so Stella may resume her singing."

She gaped at him for a moment. This was even more surprising than Blondel's offer. So many questions crowded her mind, each vying for an answer. Not just the situation with Ludlow, but their future. Jerome's sisters, like most women of their class, didn't earn a living outside the home. Would he expect the same from her?

Besides, if she should be with child…

"Well, I am glad to hear it, and I hope you are successful, *monsieur*," Blondel replied. "Perhaps you should tell me more about the operas you've performed, *madame*."

"Oh, how fascinating!" Geneviève exclaimed. "Do tell, Stella!"

Marbois sighed. "I'm afraid my taste for opera does not extend to lengthy conversations on the topic. Saint Yves, would you be interested in going for a ride? Tremblay mentioned that he'd like to give us a tour of his estate."

Jerome shifted slightly next to her. "I'm not sure…"

"Come, man, it won't take long. Perhaps it could give us ideas for my own estate."

"You should go," Stella said. "I'll return to the house with Geneviève and Monsieur Blondel, and wait for you there."

His expression carried a hint of concern, but from the way he was fidgeting with the lapel of his jacket, she could tell he was tempted. "All right. If you wait for me at the house…"

"I will, *mio amato*. I promise."

Marbois nodded. "That's settled, then. Let us go find Tremblay and get some horses saddled."

Jerome kissed Stella's temple, then followed Marbois in the direction of the house, while she continued at a more leisurely pace with Geneviève and Blondel, chatting about her time in Covent Garden. Her gaze trailed after Jerome as he stalked up the path, his muscular back straining the fabric of his jacket. *Dio santo*, this day had been perfect, yet she could hardly wait for the night to come.

When they returned, Geneviève sat down with some needlework, and Blondel joined in a game of backgammon. Stella strolled onto the terrace and leaned on the balustrade. The late afternoon sun threw shades of gold on the sloping lawns. How long had Jerome been gone? No more than an hour, and still she longed for him to return. Perhaps she should visit the library to try and distract herself.

"I saw you and Geneviève talking with Pierre Blondel. Planning on joining the Opéra Comique, are you?"

Stella turned. Marcelline had joined her on the terrace and was fanning herself with a bored pout.

"I don't see what business it is of yours," Stella retorted.

"Well, I hate to admit it, but after hearing you sing *Deh vieni non tardar,* it's no wonder you piqued Blondel's interest. At least I can be sure you will not return to the Olympique."

"A happy resolution for both of us, then."

"Just as long as we agree to equally share the stage tonight, such as it is."

Stella shrugged. "I see no reason why we couldn't. I cannot say I enjoy your company, Marcelline, but neither am I your enemy."

Marcelline snorted. "At least now you're being honest. Although, if you are not my enemy, perhaps you can lend me your chambermaid this evening. She did a good job arranging your hair yesterday, while mine made my hair look like a bird's nest."

Indeed, the chambermaid assigned to Stella, a slight, plain-faced young woman, had been the picture of quiet efficiency and was quite skilled in chignons.

"I don't see why not. Come then, let us go find her now and you can ask her yourself. It's still a bit early to get ready for dinner, but maybe she's already upstairs."

They found her in the corridor, standing near the servant's staircase and rummaging through the pocket of her apron.

Stella strode toward her. "Excuse me, miss."

The maid bowed her head and crossed her hands in front of her demurely.

"Madame Duhamel is in need of your assistance tonight. If you could accommodate her before doing my hair, that would be splendid. What sort of coiffure did you have in mind, Marcelline?"

She turned. The corridor was deserted. Marcelline was gone. In an instant, confusion turned to dread.

A hand slipped over her mouth and the sharp point of a blade dug into her back.

"One move, and you're dead."

Chapter Fifteen

THE THUDS OF Jerome's riding boots echoed through the hallways. Stella was not in the library, and now that he'd reached the conservatory, she wasn't there, either.

He stood on the threshold, gaze glancing over the room where she had sung so magnificently only last night. His heart rate accelerated, but he shook off the sensation. She had to be somewhere.

Upstairs.

He'd returned from his ride with Tremblay and Marbois, eager for her company, but she was not playing cards with Blondel, or in the sitting room with Genevieve. Was she taking a nap? Getting ready for supper? Whichever the case, he ached to hold her in his arms, feel her warm body against his, breathe in her scent.

He turned and strode above stairs to their bedchamber.

The door swung open to reveal a neatly made bed, no clothes in sight. Not the slightest sign that Stella had returned since luncheon.

For several moments, Jerome stood frozen in the doorway, his mind galloping to catch up to what his eyes saw and drawing a dire conclusion.

Gut-wrenching terror seized him. Something was wrong.

Deeply, terribly wrong. He wrestled the feeling down.

Use your head. Do not panic.

She could have gone exploring anywhere in this stately house—the gardens, another room… No. No, she'd promised she'd wait for him inside. She had absolutely no reason to traipse through random rooms by herself.

Besides which, she *knew* he would be alarmed if he could not find her. She would have left a note at the very least.

He turned and galloped down the stairs. Not a second to waste. Perhaps he was being overly cautious, but he couldn't take chances.

Out to the terrace, where Marbois and Tremblay chatted, still in their riding clothes. Marbois turned to Jerome with a smile that instantly vanished.

"*Seigneur*, what is the matter?"

He forced his breath to steady. Clear, concise words. Time was of the essence. "I cannot find Stella anywhere."

Tremblay snorted. "As you have seen, this is a large estate. Plenty of places she could be."

Blast, if the situation didn't seem so dire, he might take a few moments to bash Tremblay's teeth in.

"It's that box she sold you," he told Marbois. "I know it is. My gut tells me. The man she took it from has been after her. I have no time to explain the long and short of it, but trust me when I tell you that this is a serious matter."

Marbois frowned. "Have you looked everywhere?"

"Not the servants' quarters or the second floor."

"Then how do you know she—"

He dug his fingers into Marbois's shoulders. "Listen to me, damn you, she is in danger!"

"Excuse me, *monsieur*."

Jerome whipped around. Geneviève stole cautiously towards them, her footfalls soft as a mouse, her bubbly manner strangely sedate.

"I saw Marcelline and Stella passing by while I was in the

sitting room," she said. "Around half an hour ago. I couldn't hear what they were saying, but they seemed to be heading towards the stairs."

"The stairs," Jerome repeated, pushing Marbois away. "And you did not see them come down?"

Geneviève shook her head, her eyes wide and fearful. "Has something happened to Stella?"

Marbois took her hand. "Don't fret, my sweet, I'm sure this is all a misunderstanding."

A misunderstanding. Jerome's mind worked furiously. No. No, it was more than that. This house was full of people, guests and servants. If someone had taken Stella out of here, they had to have planned it. Carefully. And that plan must involve more than one conspirator.

And who was the last person to have seen Stella? Someone with potential motive to wish her harm, if only to be rid of a rival.

"Tremblay, what room are Madame Duhamel and Monsieur Girard staying in?"

"Second door on the left. But surely you don't mean to—"

He rushed back to the stairs.

"What do you think they know?" Marbois trailed after him. "You can't seriously think you can barge in there and interrogate her."

"Try and stop me."

His feet thundered on the steps and thumped on the thick carpet of the corridor, with Marbois close behind. He pounded on the finely decorated panel. "Open. Open at once."

A shriek came from the other side, followed by some muffled curses.

The door opened just enough for Girard's face to appear. "What is the meaning of this?"

Jerome shoved at the wood panel, pushing the fleshy man into the room along with it.

"I demand an explanation," Girard spluttered, his jowls jiggling.

Jerome ignored him. Marcelline sat in front of her mirror in her peignoir, her hair loose on her shoulders.

She gasped and clutched at the front of her peignoir, drawing the bodice close to her throat. "How dare you, *monsieur!*"

"Spare me your false indignation," he snapped. "Where is Stella?"

"How on earth should I know?"

"Geneviève told us she saw you with her," Marbois said.

Jerome stepped closer. "You were heading to the stairs, but she has not come down, and now she's disappeared. *Where is she?*"

She lifted her chin, though her gaze flitted away. "I don't have the faintest idea. Really, with the number of staircases in this place, you can't possibly expect me to keep track of her."

"There, she's answered you," Girard spat. "Now get out of our room, you lout!"

The shrew was lying, damn her, and attempting to playact her way out of it. Fury boiled dangerously close to the surface, but he could hardly beat the truth out of her.

"You refuse to tell me the truth, *madame*. Very well. I will simply have to fill in the missing parts myself. You schemed to dispose of a rival because you were jealous of her superior talent."

She waved a hand. "Superior talent. Really."

"Anyone who heard her sing last night can attest to it. At any rate, you arranged for her to come here before setting a trap. I wonder how many invitations you will receive if my wife comes to harm and rumors start to spread about who the culprit is."

"Who do you think would believe you?" she sniffed.

"Pierre Blondel for one. And I have no doubt the director of the Opéra Comique will believe him."

Marcelline's face paled, yet still, she protested. "He is nothing to me."

"What a boon for him too," Jerome continued. "The *prima donna* of a rival theater, resorting to felony in order to secure her position. It might make its way to the *Gazette*."

She laughed, but it rang hollow. "You think your wife is so

important this news will make the newspapers?"

"*You* are, in any case," Marbois quipped. "There is but one small step from famous to notorious, and the public does enjoy a scandal."

Marcelline crossed her arms and tapped her foot. "Fine. I will tell you what happened. But she brought this on herself. Bianca Romano, ha! I could tell as soon as I met her that she was trouble. Deceitful little bitch."

Devil take it, he had never laid a hand on a woman, but his palm itched to strike her cheek. "Watch your mouth, or your lover will be eating supper without his teeth."

Behind him, Girard emitted a faint whimper.

"After Tremblay told us about his party," she continued, "a man approached me. He said he would pay me if I could get Stella to attend. And that is the end of my involvement."

"Bloody hell, you told Geneviève that it would be a good idea for her to come and sing," Marbois exclaimed. "And then Geneviève mentioned as much to me."

A carefully prepared plan indeed. This must have been weeks ago. To think of what he was up against…

"I could hardly invite her myself," Marcelline replied. "I had to find a way. The sum was… quite significant."

"Significant?" Jerome asked. "Merely to get her to attend a party? There had to be more."

She sighed. "Then I was supposed to wait for instructions. Right after you all went off riding, Stella's chambermaid told me to bring her upstairs, near the entrance of the servants' staircase."

Her chambermaid? Not his idea of a hardened criminal, but that was precisely the point. A domestic would blend in naturally, and a maid was the last person who would arouse suspicion.

He thought he'd taken precautions. Whoever was playing this cruel game was several steps ahead of them.

"Before you ask again, I don't know where your wife is," Marcelline muttered. "All I know is that they're taking her straight to Calais. Apparently, she's wanted for robbery back in

England."

Marbois grunted. "Of course. Right back over the Channel. They could be there in three days."

Jerome shook his head. It did make sense, but something niggled at him. Clearly Marcelline was only a pawn. Why bother to tell her what they were planning on doing with Stella?

Unless…

Unless they were counting on Marcelline to feed them this information, as a means to throw him off Stella's track. They weren't taking her to Calais. But then where…

You think you can take down the Kingfisher. He's got men on his payroll from Cherbourg to Dunkirk.

The Kingfisher. A river bird. The Kingfisher and his smugglers must operate on the Seine before distributing to different ports. And the river was at hand, the nearest bend ten kilometers south.

Ten kilometers. An hour's easy ride, but night would soon fall. And he hadn't the slightest idea where to look once he reached the river. But God help him, if they took Stella in a boat, he would never find her again.

He pushed back a fresh wave of anguish and turned to Marbois. "Tell Tremblay I'm taking his horse."

EVERY BONE IN Stella's body ached, but it was nothing compared to the agony of not knowing when the jostling would stop. She lay in the hard, wooden bed of a wagon, shoved into a tiny space between crates, and she felt every rut in the road down to her bones. But stopping would be worse, because what awaited her then…

The wheel hit a rock and reeled on. Pain vibrated through her limbs, and she whimpered against the rough cloth covering her mouth. She stared ahead, but there was nothing to see but the gray burlap they'd thrown over her, the last light of day making the threads barely distinguishable. Darkness, soon. Utter darkness.

Porca miseria, how would Jerome find her?

Panic rose in her chest and cut her breath short. No escape, no way to flee. No hope.

Stop. Gather your wits.

For now, she could only try to piece together what had happened. Whoever Ludlow had enlisted to take her had executed a masterful plan. She would never have suspected the fine-boned chambermaid could subdue her and drag her down the servants' staircase. But the woman had twisted Stella's arm, holding it against her back as they moved together, applying just enough pressure to show Stella she could break her wrist or pop her elbow out of its socket. If she didn't plunge the blade into her back first.

Then the maid had led her through a deserted part of the courtyard to a small side entrance of the estate. A wagon had been waiting for them near the road, driven by a man in plain clothes.

They'd bound her hands and feet, tied a cloth over her mouth, thrown her on the floor of the wagon between two rows of crates and covered her with a moldy-smelling burlap sack. She was goods to be delivered, nothing more.

Fear twisted her insides. She fought to contain it, but it was like fending off a swarm of venomous insects.

Of course, Jerome would notice her absence the moment he got back. He would know she was in danger. He would interrogate that *stronza*, and he would come for her.

Alone, against these criminals… Tears rose to her eyes. Perhaps it was better if he didn't find her. He would take care of Clara…

No. No. Do not think of her.

The wagon slowed as the road became rougher, then finally lurched to a stop. Silence, then two voices muttering to each other. Silence again, deep and undisturbed save for the faint rustling of grass.

"Unload the cart." A third voice, low and commanding. "The woman first."

The burlap was torn away. Above her, a canopy of leaves hid the night sky. A pair of arms lifted her and deposited her on the ground, cutting the bonds at her feet.

The driver held a lantern while two other men unloaded the cart. A gaunt man with a dark wide-brimmed hat watched her. *Inspecting* her. His cold, indifferent gaze traveled over her without betraying the slightest flicker of interest or emotion.

"Unhurt as promised, Kingfisher," the driver said. "Emelise got her without a hitch, and no one followed us on the road."

"Good. He's waiting inside."

The black swarm engulfed her, drowned her, and nausea tore through her belly. Who was *he*? Not him. It couldn't be. Please God, anyone but him.

The Kingfisher wrapped his fingers around her arm, tight as a vise, and pushed her forward. A tiny path led downward through thick woods. Not a house in sight. She could scream her lungs ragged and no one would hear.

The trees gave way to a small clearing. In the middle stood a windowless warehouse. And just beyond the grassy riverbank, two large rowboats were moored on wooden stakes.

The Seine. Despair pierced her heart. If they put her on one of those boats, she would never see Jerome or Clara ever again.

Grip relentless, the Kingfisher guided her into the house. A single, large room with a high ceiling, packed with crates, barrels and sacks. In one corner, several men sat at a table, speaking in muted voices, lantern light flickering in their faces. One of them bolted upright. A tall frame, greasy blond hair slicked back…

Her nightmare come to life.

Stella's knees nearly gave way, but the Kingfisher's implacable grip kept her on her feet.

The Marquess of Ludlow slowly advanced, his mouth twisted in a vicious smile.

"Well, my dear Miss Cardinelli," he said, "I've had a devil of a time getting you back. *Mille mercis*, Kingfisher."

His clipped, aristocratic English couldn't hide the cold, cruel undertones of his voice. He took another step and grazed the side of her face with his forefinger. She struggled against her bonds, her heart hammering in her ribcage like a trapped bird trying to take flight.

"I have sadly not been successful retrieving my box, despite having come in person to this wretched country, but I daresay you will make a nice consolation prize. One I plan to enjoy the entire way back to England, before I let others have a go."

The bold-faced arrogance in his tone, his falsely playful manner.... Precisely what had repulsed her from the outset. He spoke to all women that way.

He had spoken to Lilian in those tones, no doubt, just before shattering her innocence.

A wild flare of fury roared to life, and the blackness receded in its wake. She screamed against the cloth. Ludlow merely laughed.

"What do you have to say for yourself, you wicked girl?"

He shoved the cloth down, and she took a deep breath through her mouth.

"*Cazzo si, pezzo di merda,*" she snarled, tugging furiously at the rope digging into her wrists. "I should have used a stronger poison on you and rid the earth of your stench."

"Yes, perhaps," he replied, almost amused. "Did you seriously think I would not find you? You're a *singer*. Barely better than a disease-ridden harlot. And I am a peer of the realm."

"By the night's end, you will be nothing more than a rotting corpse."

She spat in his face. His smile evaporated. A slap seared her cheek and her head whipped back.

"You fucking whore." He wiped the saliva dripping down his cheek with his sleeve. "No one is coming to save you, least of all that pathetic lobcock you spread your legs for. I must admit, I don't usually take the leavings of commoners, but in your case,

I'll make an exception."

He shoved the cloth back into place over her mouth and nodded towards the Kingfisher. "Put her in the cache, that ought to subdue her. And tell your men to hurry up and load those damned boats."

Chapter Sixteen

J EROME PULLED UP on the reins, and patted the horse's neck. "Woah, boy."

His mount was soaked, its great lungs heaving like a bellows. Jerome had pushed the beast until the bank of the Seine appeared on the horizon.

The last purple hues of sunset were fast fading, and until the moon rose, he would have to slow to a walk. The desperate energy in his belly kicked against his ribcage, but it would do Stella little good if he broke his neck or maimed his mount. Every minute that passed lessened his chances of catching up with his wife's abductors.

And there was another problem. He squinted at the cross-roads in the distance. If he continued south, he would reach Épinay, on the banks of the river. But east or west would bring him farther upstream or downstream. It was like drawing straws and selecting one of three haystacks in which to search for a needle.

Get yourself together, man. No time to feel sorry for himself. The quickest route to the Seine was through Épinay, and he had to reach the river first and foremost. Straight on, then.

As he drew closer, he could make out a stone cross standing tall and imposing on the roadside. A man sat on the plinthe, holding the reins of a horse. A shiver ran down Jerome's spine and his fingers gave a sharp tug to stop his mount. He had been told as a boy that crossroads were cursed places, where one might meet the devil in disguise. Jerome was not so wary of the devil as he was of lawless men.

"Aren't you going to come and greet a friend, Saint Yves?"

That voice. *Impossible.* He pressed the flanks of the horse. Smiling, the man leaped to his feet, blond curls peaking from under a dark, flat cap.

"Lefevre, what the bloody hell are you doing here?"

"Waiting for you, obviously."

Blast, those tales about the devil might be true, after all. "How did you know…?"

"Let us discuss this while we ride. I imagine you don't want to waste time. We've got a kingfisher to catch." He mounted his horse. "Take the road on the right."

Lefevre spurred his horse until the two could set off together. For once, he had traded his extravagant waistcoats for plain, dark clothes. A man on a mission, the very same as Jerome.

"Explain, then. You know they've taken Stella?"

"I figured as much," Lefevre replied in a grim tone. "Today I got word that the Kingfisher was planning on leaving his hideout with his men tonight. I also learned that a few weeks past he struck a deal with the Bone Man in order to snatch Stella from Tremblay's party."

Jerome nodded. "Her chambermaid was in on it, if you can believe it."

"Oh, I believe it. In fact, I suspect I know who the Bone Man sent on the job, and if it's who I think, Stella was wise not to make a run for it."

"Who told you about the deal?"

Lefevre hesitated. "A reliable source. That's also how I know where the Kingfisher's hideout is. The information came too late for me to ride all the way to Tremblay's estate and warn you, but I trusted you would make your way here, one way or another. I told the others I would wait until nightfall on the road going south from Montmorency."

Jerome nodded. "Thank you, Lefevre. I am in your debt."

"Wait until your wife is safe in your arms, then we can discuss what you owe me."

Safe in his arms. By God, how he ached for her, a relentless, grinding need that both spurred him on and held his chest in a cold grip. But he had a guide now, at least, and a second pair of hands.

"I should warn you, I am unarmed," he said. "I would not trust myself firing a pistol in the dead of night. I would risk harming myself as much as my opponent."

"I detest the damn things," Lefevre muttered. "Some of the others brought firepower, but for me, nothing beats a solid fist and a sharp blade."

"The others? Which *others*?"

Instead of replying, Lefevre turned onto a smaller road leading down a slope towards the wood. At the edge of the trees, pistol in hand, a burly man watched over four horses.

Jerome's heart thudded faster. "Is this one of your others, Lefevre?"

"The pair of us are not enough to take on the Kingfisher and his acolytes. I had to agree to some… help."

His tone was strangely bitter, but Jerome had no choice. He must trust Lefevre. The only thing that mattered was finding Stella.

Nicolas nodded at the man, then dismounted and tied the reins of his horse to a branch. Jerome followed suit.

"The Kingfisher's hideout is less than a kilometer east, on the banks of the river. Stay close behind me, as quietly as you can."

As soon as they entered the woods, they were engulfed in darkness. Jerome treaded cautiously, but Lefevre walked faster, as if his senses allowed him to move with ease in the dark, and Jerome had to quicken his pace, though roots and rocks insisted on placing themselves in his path. Soon the moon filtered through the leaves, making their passage easier.

"Full moon," Lefevre said in a hushed tone. "If the Kingfisher is on the move, someone else is giving him orders."

They continued in silence for a few minutes, then Lefevre stopped. He emitted a short, trilling whistle like a bird call, paused, then did it again. A second later, a similar call answered.

They crept closer until Jerome could make out the outlines of a house in a clearing. No windows, no chimney. A warehouse, then. Faint firelight flickered through cracks between the wooden planks. Even in this faint light, he could tell it was poorly built. Quick to erect, and quick to tear down.

He crouched next to Lefevre. His heart hammered ever faster, his limbs trembled with the impulse to spring and tear down the door. Tear those men apart for harming Stella.

Get her back. He must get her back immediately.

Lefevre touched his shoulder, as if sensing his restlessness. "Wait for the signal," he whispered. "Then head straight inside and find Stella. Leave the fighting to us."

Seconds ticked by, and with them the last of his resolve to remain still. Finally, the warehouse door opened, and three smugglers emerged, carrying sacks on their shoulders and heading towards the boats moored on the bank. Another call sounded, low and melodious like that of an owl.

Leaves rustled and twigs snapped.

Lefevre tugged on Jerome's sleeve. "Now."

Jerome sprang to his feet and pelted towards the clearing, blood pounding in his ears, fists at the ready. Other men melted out of the forest, advancing towards the warehouse. One of the smugglers caught sight of them and yelled. The blast of a gunshot tore through the night, followed by a loud splash.

Jerome ran. On the threshold, an unseen force knocked him to the ground sending the air from his lungs. A fist connected with his jaw making bursts of light explode before his eyes. He grabbed his assailant's collar and flung him aside. The man landed on his back with a grunt, and Jerome scrambled to his feet, kicking him square in the stomach before rushing to the door.

Inside was pandemonium. Another shot exploded, closer to him this time. He caught a glimpse of Nicolas fending off an opponent, a man with a dark hat, his blade flashing.

Stella. He must find Stella.

He could only see barrels, crates. Men grappling, throwing fists. Cries and shouts filled his ears.

"Where is she?" he roared, anger and frustration and despair boiling over.

A tall, blond man staggered towards the door. Trying to escape. Jerome rounded on him and grabbed his arm.

"You. Where did they hide Stella?"

"I… I do not know," the man stammered, his voice carrying the hint of an accent.

Jerome shook him. "Tell me where they put my wife, or I will tear you limb to limb, you whoreson."

The man's eyes widened, and a wild laugh burst from his mouth. "You. It's you. Risking your life for that little slut. Stupid sod."

He spoke in English. Perfect English. Crisp and elegant. Refined. Aristocratic.

Ludlow.

Before Jerome would make sense of his presence, a stinging, acrid smell filled his nostrils, and a vivid glow danced at the edge of his vision.

Fire. One of the crates was on fire.

Jerome's grip slackened for half a moment, and Ludlow tore away from him. Jerome picked up a sack and hurled it at him. It caught him in the back of the head, and he crumpled to the ground. Jerome's gaze darted around, searching for a plank, his veins pulsing with frenzied fury, with the impulse to kill, to bash the bastard's face in until nothing was left but pulverized flesh.

"Jerome! The barrels! They're marked!"

He whipped around.

Lefevre brandished his knife, and blood stained the front of his shirt. "Gunpowder," he cried. "There isn't much time!"

The fire was burning through the crates now, its flames licking up towards the ceiling. Either from the gunpowder or the ceiling, the entire warehouse would soon collapse.

Stella. Lord have mercy, where had they hidden her?

Smugglers. They must have hiding places to conceal the most precious goods. In the walls? No, they were too thin. Hastily built. Letting firelight through the cracks.

The floor.

"She's under the floor," he yelled at Lefevre.

Where? He couldn't tear it apart plank by plank. His gaze darted to and fro, searching, looking, sweat running down his forehead. The heat was unbearable, the air thick with smoke. Hurry, he must hurry.

There. A row of planks not quite aligned with the rest. A centimeter at most.

"Give me your knife!" he yelled to Lefevre. "A blade! Anything!"

Lefevre handed him a thick butcher's knife. Jerome wedged in the blade between the two rows of planks and lifted until he could slide his fingers underneath. He crouched and pulled up. Pulled even though the wood cut into the flesh of his fingers and tore his skin. Pulled until the wood ceded with a loud crack.

He saw her eyes first. Round and filled with fear, like a trapped animal. Her mouth covered and her hands bound. Lying in a space as narrow as a coffin.

Relief washed over him like a great wave. He couldn't speak. He could only grab her shoulders and the back of her knees and lift her, his muscles straining and his lungs struggling for breath. No matter. She was in his arms now. Alive. Trembling, frightened, but alive. He shoved down the cloth tied around her face, freeing her mouth.

"Jerome," she rasped. "Jerome..."

The men still standing were fleeing from the inferno now. The flames everywhere, biting into the wood of the barrels. From the corner of his eye, he could see Ludlow moving, trying to get back up on his feet.

He ran. Reached the door. Filled his lungs with fresh air.

"Over here!" Lefevre called. He was almost at the edge of the trees.

Jerome ran faster. A moment later, a terrific blast filled the night and knocked him to the ground. He shielded Stella with his body for several seconds before looking up and catching his breath.

"*Sacredieu*," Lefevre said. "What a show. Here, set her hands free."

Jerome lay Stella down in the grass and took Lefevre's switchblade to cut the rope binding her wrists.

Her eyelids fluttered open. "Jerome…"

He stroked her hair. "Speak to me, my love. Are you hurt?"

She coughed, then her lips curled into a little smile and raised her hand to his cheek. "I am fine, now. I knew you would find me, *mio amato*. My beloved."

He kissed her palm. Tears blurred his vision and ran down his cheeks to wet her fingers. "No one will ever take you from me again. Ever, do you hear?"

She nodded. "He cannot harm us anymore. You, me or Clara."

"Yes. Yes, we will stay together, always." He leaned down to place a gentle kiss on her lips. "We need to get out of here. Lefevre, can you…"

Lefevre laughed. "Oh, for heaven's sake, man, call me Nicolas."

NICOLAS WATCHED JEROME ride away, Stella propped in front of him. A strong constitution, that one, with a temper to match. When Jerome had suggested they search for a carriage in Épinay, she'd outright refused.

"I am well enough to ride with you," she'd insisted. "Let us go back to Tremblay's without delay. I am in desperate need of a bath and a clean bed, and in desperate need to tell Marcelline that she is the vilest, most heinous woman I have ever had the misfortune to meet."

The night air was cool and clear with moonlight. They would reach Montmorency before dawn. Shame he couldn't accompany them and see the rest of Stella's performance for himself.

"So, you got rid of the Kingfisher yourself, eh?" Talloche asked.

He turned to the barrel-chested man. Part of Talloche's face bore the rippling scars of a burn. A fighter who had paid his dues in the past.

"Those were Malenfant's orders," Nicolas replied shortly. And he'd had to use his blade too, after his opponent had pulled his butcher's knife. Messy business. "He didn't help me out of the goodness of his heart, though any one of you thugs could have killed the Kingfisher."

"Indeed. Suppose he was trying to see if you had the guts to do it."

Nicolas raised an eyebrow. "Do you think me a fool? That's not what he was about."

A gravelly laugh rumbled in Talloche's throat. "The Kingfisher struck a deal with the Bone Man. Now you'll be on the Bone Man's list. If you worked for Malenfant, you wouldn't have to worry about ending up in the catacombs." His mouth curled in a sinister smile. "Parts of you, at least."

"I don't take sides," Nicolas snapped. "I owe your master a favor now, but that's as far as it goes."

And damn him, he would not have done this had he any other choice. But he and Jerome couldn't have saved Stella without Malenfant's men. Saving an innocent from an abominable fate and helping the brother-in-law of a dear friend was worth being in Malenfant's debt.

Just as long as Malenfant didn't think Nicolas would join his merry bands of criminals.

"You can tell him Ludlow is dead," he added. "That ought to please the box's new owner. I suppose that for someone who dines weekly with Bonaparte, it comes in handy to have the likes of Malenfant to do the dirty work."

Talloche slapped Nicolas's back. "You're just as dirty as the rest of us, Lefevre. Better put your skills to use if you know what's good for you."

Not if the devil himself asked him. He'd gone down that path before, and knew where it led. Never again would he become another man's lackey.

"Well, Malenfant knows where to find me," Nicolas said with a smile. "He can come down to Palais Royal anytime. Perhaps I can give him a little lesson in savate."

Chapter Seventeen

STELLA AWOKE WITH a start, heart racing.

She stared in confusion at her surroundings. The room was plunged in murky dimness, not quite the darkness of the night nor the pale light of dawn. Her gaze flitted from the fireplace to the table to the door. All unfamiliar to her.

Then the last remnants of her dream fell away, and she remembered. The inn. This was their room at the inn. They were on their way to Chartres.

She turned, drawn to the comforting heat at her side. Jerome lay on his back, his bare chest rising and falling in slow, even rhythm, his features smooth and sharp as a marble sculpture.

Stella smiled and grazed his cheekbone with the back of her fingers. In the three weeks since the rescue, nightmares had regularly disturbed her sleep, warped sensations of being trapped in a dark place with no way out, or visions of a fire spreading. But they all melted away the moment she realized she was safe in bed with her husband.

Safe. Yes, Ludlow was dead. Nothing remained of him. And she was alive, cherished and cared for. Loved.

Jerome rolled to his side. She nestled closer, her back to his chest. His arms circled her waist, still heavy and sluggish with sleep. Rain pattered softly against the window pane. She closed her eyes, ready to drift back into slumber, surrounded by warmth.

Jerome moved again, and his leg slid over hers, hitching up her nightrail. They were completely entwined now, and a familiar warmth flickered to life, tugging between her legs, chasing all thoughts of slumber from her mind. Would he be terribly mad if she woke him? Perhaps annoyed at first, until she explained the reason for her restlessness…

His arm tightened around her, and he burrowed his face in her hair. Ah, maybe she did not need to wake him after all. She arched her hips against him. One part of him, at least, was rousing quickly.

She rolled her backside against his growing erection in a slow, languorous movement. Jerome groaned and his hands came alive on her body, one of them kneading her breast through the thin linen, the other lifting the hem of her nightrail to cup between her legs. Liquid heat pooled at his touch, and he ran two fingers along the crease, swirling, teasing, pressing against her sheath.

"Spread your legs wider, my love," he rumbled hoarsely against her ear.

The low, commanding pitch of his voice sent a shudder of yearning through her belly. She lifted her knee, and his fingers plunged into her, sinking deep before easing out again, unfurling a wave of white-hot sensation. One, two, three more times, slowly. Too slowly. *Dio santo*, this was unendurable. She grasped his wrist, trying to make him move faster, and felt him smile against her temple.

His touch abated.

"Jerome," she moaned, "what are you doing?"

But she was too aroused to be fully exasperated. Would he make her beg? The thought spurred on her desire to an alarming degree.

"I want you naked," he rasped.

Two could play that game. With deliberate languidness, she made her nightrail slide up her torso, over her breasts. Chest heaving, he followed her movements with a burning gaze. When finally she tossed the nightrail asides, he grasped her hips, tilting them back. Then guided the head of his manhood to her entrance, and thrust his thick length into her. A sharp cry burst from her lips.

His pace was quick. Quick and relentless, heightening her need with each vigorous thrust.

"Yes, please, do not stop, *please,*" she panted helplessly.

"More?" he growled.

"God, yes, give me more."

He pounded harder. She was close, so close… He slapped her thigh, the searing sting bringing her higher still. She cried out, and his palm met her soft flesh again. She soared, toppled, drowned in a flood of pleasure. His thrusts sharpened until his fingers dug into her skin, and he shook against her, calling her name.

She let herself relax against him, cradled in his arms. They lay still for a few moments, until Jerome gently slid out of her, his hot seed seeping onto her legs. She turned around and their mouths met in a kiss.

"Good morning," he said in a teasing voice. "Did you sleep well?"

She stretched, arching her spine. "I much prefer the way I woke up."

His eyes clouded with concern. "Nightmares?"

"Yes, but I don't really remember," she replied with a sigh. "I just awoke with an unpleasant feeling."

"It will pass in time, my love. I had nightmares most every night after we fled the Terror. Antonia as well, she would wake up screaming and crying. But eventually, the nightmares receded." He stroked her cheek. "All is well now. We are together. Next month, God willing, you will return to the stage."

Thanks to Pierre Blondel, who was now a frequent visitor in rue Castellane, along with his very dear friend the director of the Opéra Comique. Every day that passed and brought her closer to performing was one day closer to feeling free again. All the fears she had battled, all the joy that filled her now—she would be able to express it in her singing.

"And in a matter of hours," Jerome added, "you will be reunited with Clara."

That longing tugged at her heart with even greater force. "Oh, I cannot wait to see her again. Such blasted luck yesterday."

If everything had gone as planned, they would have arrived yesterday, but rain and mud had slowed the carriage. At dusk twenty kilometers still lay between them and Honorine's house. Though a wise decision, stopping for the night meant a painful delay of the moment she would see Clara again.

Every three or four days, a letter from Honorine had reassured them of the baby's good health. Her coos and smiles charmed the entire family, and Jane was in excellent spirits and well on her way to learning French.

Honorine's kindness warmed Stella's heart. No doubt she could perfectly understand the apprehensions of a young mother separated from her child. But reading about Clara playing with her cousins or learning to pick up wooden blocks with her tiny hands only made Stella miss her more.

Soon. Soon they would be together, and then, for the first time in her life, her happiness would be complete.

"Come then, let us get dressed," Jerome said. "We will leave as soon as we've had breakfast, and arrive in time for luncheon."

They kissed again, and Stella sat up. "Listen, Jerome."

"What is it? I hear nothing."

"Exactly." She grinned at him over her shoulder. "It finally stopped raining."

JEROME BREATHED IN the scent of wet grass and looked at the hills that stretched beyond the road. Shades of soft green and burnished yellow, patches of trees between gentle slopes, and the

August sun blazing in a cloudless sky. The colors of home. The light was different here, somehow, though he could not put that difference into words. The familiarity both appeased and unsettled him.

"The carriage will soon be ready to go."

He turned towards Stella. "You are utterly ravishing, my love."

She laughed, though a pretty blush dotted her cheeks. "Silly man, I have worn the same traveling costume since we left Paris."

He took her hand and drew her near. "Still, that shade of blue is perfect for you. And the matching ribbon on your hat…"

She planted her fist on her hip. "Don't you dare say it."

"… which you sewed *yourself* is lovely as well."

"Only because Jane was not there," she replied, swatting his chest. "Don't get used to me doing any needlework, especially as I am so wretched at it. Your sister will notice the uneven stitches."

"She will be so overjoyed to meet you, I doubt she will pay much attention to your hat."

"I do hope you're right."

He lifted her chin to look into her eyes. "Are you nervous?"

She gave him a half-smile. "A little, yes. Aren't you?"

He turned his gaze back towards the hill and nodded. "Honorine is younger, but she is a mother six times over, whereas I… I have not yet learned to take care of a family. I keep thinking that, somehow, I might fall short."

"*Mio amato.*" Stella rested her head against his shoulder. "You worked hard so your family could survive when you were in London. Then you took me and Clara in, protected us, saved me from a gang of criminals. And yet, after all this, you are still afraid to fail those you love. Why?"

He sighed. "Coming here brings back memories. As a young man, I was not so dutiful. In fact, I… I strayed, when I was seventeen or so. I suppose most boys that age do, but in my case, it had disastrous consequences."

Stella stroked his arm and waited for him to continue.

"Annette was the daughter of a farmer who lived close by. My father raised me to treat gentlewomen with the utmost courtesy and never to accost members of our domestic staff, but beyond that… It is expected for young men to find an outlet to their impulses. My friends certainly thought nothing of it. And Annette seemed… receptive to my attention."

Round rosy cheeks, dark brown hair, a pretty smile that lit up every time their eyes met… Yes, he could still picture how she'd looked back then, before everything unraveled.

"We were both inexperienced, but managed to meet a few times in places we thought hidden from view. However, one evening, her father caught us and…" He swallowed. "He beat her there in front of me and called her all sorts of terrible names. I intervened, but he told me he had every right to chastise his daughter. Like she was his property, no better than chattel. So I fought him. Or, at least I tried. I was no match for a full-grown man who spent all day in the fields."

"You have certainly changed in that respect," Stella said, her tone chiding and soft.

"Well, he did quick work of me. One punch to the jaw sent me reeling," He shook his head. "And when I got home, I was too ashamed to tell my parents. They saw my bruise, and I said I had fallen from my horse."

"What happened to Annette?"

That was the worst part, by far. "Her father married her off to another farmer. For a few weeks, I agonized over whether I had gotten her with child, but I guess it was simply to keep her out of trouble. A year later, we passed on the road. By then she was indeed expecting her first child, but the way she looked at me… It was as if I had failed to step up and save her."

Her eyes had been full of despair, brimming with tears. Was she in love with him? Was her husband a violent man? By the time he had built up the courage to ask around, his own world had fallen to pieces. His parents had succumbed to disease, the

Terror had started, and everything he had known as a boy had been swept away.

"When we returned from London, her entire family was gone. Who can tell what became of her?"

Stella stroked his arm, soothing him with her tenderness. "It was such a long time ago, *mio amato*. You were foolish, yes, but her father was the one who treated her cruelly. He is the real culprit here."

He turned away, and they drifted in the direction of the carriage. "That's what I tried to tell myself. Still, I wanted to be a man like my father. Responsible, loyal, honest. And now that I… that I have started a family, I am afraid I will not live up to his name."

Stella stopped and took both his hands. "Jerome Saint Yves, look at me. Look at me." She waited for him to comply before going on. "If I thought for a moment that you could not be a worthy father, I would not let you near Clara." She squeezed his fingers. "You told me that the circumstances of Clara's birth did not matter, that I was her mother. And you were right. But Clara will have a father as well. An admirable man, hard-working and intelligent, who will do everything in his power to make her happy."

His throat tightened until speech became impossible. By God, he couldn't put into words how much he adored this woman, how she reached deep inside him and brought only what was good and true and brave to the surface.

"Yes," he managed. "Yes, my love."

She stood on tiptoe to kiss him and smiled. "Come, I think the carriage is ready."

During the trip to Chartres, Stella's words echoed in his head throughout. *A worthy father.* He would stop at nothing to become that man. For Stella, for Clara, for their future children. Would he succeed? And would he convince his sisters and their husbands, once they learned the truth about Clara's parentage, that he was a father in more than just name? Yes. Yes, they would support him.

He must not let his doubts crush his reason.

He took Stella's hand and she entwined her fingers with his. The unrest in his chest eased somewhat.

Only to start up again when the carriage rolled to a stop. Blast, he had never been this agitated walking to the door of the Saint Yves home.

He rang. A servant opened, but before she could even greet him, a cheerful exclamation resounded behind her.

Honorine swept into the corridor, arms outstretched to embrace him. "Brother! Here you are at last!"

"It's good to be here." He kissed her on both cheeks. "The rain delayed our journey somewhat."

Honorine turned to Stella and took her hand. "And how wonderful to meet you. Welcome, welcome. Oh, look who it is!"

Jane appeared, carrying Clara. "'Ere's your mum, little lady. 'Appy to see her, ain't you?"

By God, in just a few short weeks, the babe had changed. She was chubbier, her eyes more vivid, her mouth more expressive. Stella let out a strangled sob and rushed to take her in her arms, tears streaming down her face.

"There, ma'am, she's fine, as you can see," Jane said, though her voice was watery as well. "'Earty appetite, that one. Country air did 'er a load o'good."

Stella nodded, sniffling. "I can see that, yes. Here, *cara mia*, come and greet your papa."

She brought Clara to Jerome. He stood frozen. What should he do? He had held Honorine's children before, but Clara… Stella had never let him hold her. And he had never dared to ask.

"Go on," Stella murmured, her eyes brimming with love. "It's all right."

He took the baby delicately in his arms. His heart clenched painfully, wonderfully. No, this was not like holding his nieces and nephews. A new depth of tender affection he did not know even existed burst within.

Clara Saint Yves. Little Clara.

His worries melted away. He would learn. He would face every challenge head on. He would do it for his daughter. His wife. The family he had always hoped for. The family he had finally come home to. The family he would never be parted from again.

THE END

ABOUT THE AUTHOR

Twenty years after studying history at the Sorbonne, Delphine Roy put her classwork to good use in her spicy historical romances set in Post-Revolutionary France. Before that, she spent a good part of her childhood on both sides of the Atlantic and started writing stories in French and English. Her teenage self may have posted them in online fanfiction forums that thankfully no longer exist.

Delphine now lives in the suburbs of Paris with her husband and her son. She's a high school ESL teacher by day and an author by night of romance (in English) and fantasy (in French). In her free time, she enjoys cross-stitching, watching hockey and going down Wikipedia wormholes.